The Dragon's Quests

Brian Williams

 New Generation Publishing

The Old World

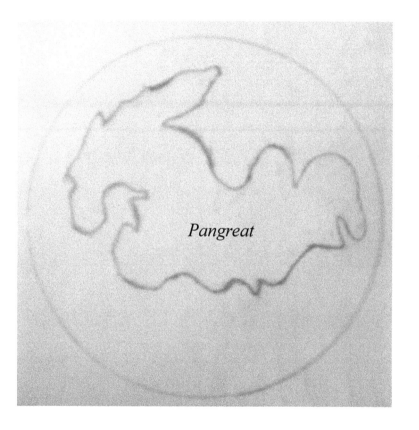

Chapter One

The Discovery

A long time ago in the old world before the dark ages, there lived a strange, green three-headed dragon. It started its life as an egg and was discovered by a farmer called Miller; the egg was partially hidden under a bush on his farm, and he noticed the egg after the sun had gone down and it was starting to get dark. Miller was drawn to the egg by the small amount of light the shell emitted.

He had to bend down so low to investigate the egg, he ended up crawling on his hands and knees – he stretched out both arms and took hold of the egg, his heart pounding with both exertion and excitement as he held the strange egg with trembling hands. "It's the biggest egg I've ever seen," he thought aloud.

He studied it closely and marvelled at the faint green light which seemed to be coming from deep inside the egg.

What had laid it? He wasn't sure – he knew there were a great many mystical creatures which inhabited the land including dragons, but where it had come from didn't trouble him at all. Without further consideration, he crawled back out from under the bush and stood up wrapping the egg in an old sack and clutching it close to his chest, as if he was cradling a baby, he started to carry it home.

Some might think this was a silly, even a dangerous thing to do, taking home a strange unknown egg, but Miller had felt no fear; in fact, he was excited and got a little out of breath as he carried the egg, being very careful to make sure he didn't stumble on the uneven ground.

He walked into the farmhouse, and unwrapping the egg, he manipulated it so that when he placed it gently down beside the warm chimney breast, it was snuggled in the sack, which resembled a small nest.

The fact that Miller was one hundred and seventy years old, had little or no effect on his decision, because sometimes age can make one hesitant and indecisive but; he was just compelled to do it.

Later that night, he tossed and turned in his bed and couldn't go to sleep, thoughts of the egg running through his mind, as he worried about his compulsive decision. Suddenly, a confident feeling overcame him and he was sure he had done something important. On reflection, it seemed as if the egg had been calling to him.

He had never experienced these emotions of fulfilment and satisfaction before. A sense of calm overcame him and he closed his eyes and drifted off into a blissful sleep. When he awoke the following morning, he was refreshed and rested.

Miller was not considered to be very old for those times, because nature ruled the world and it was a powerful force, always trying to keep a balance. Because there were so few humans on earth, nature endowed them with very long lives. If people looked after themselves, they could live to be over two hundred and seventy years and even older.

As Miller got older he was beginning to look more like his mother; with black hair and brown eyes, he had her high cheekbones and slim pointed nose – he even had her small ears. He was very tall and slim, which came from his father and walked with the same swaying motion. He also had his father's voice – deep and clear.

Unfortunately, Miller's parents had died when he was eighteen years old. Both of his parents had been very thoughtful and believed Miller needed to be independent with the ability to look after himself. From the time when he was a very small boy, they taught him everything he would need to know to survive on his own on the farm.

He became skilled in all the tasks which needed to be done around the farm, and he enjoyed watching the crops growing and loved to cook his meals from the food he produced. He was content enough living on his own, but was always happy to welcome anyone who came to barter. Most of the time he was in the company of the animals on the farm, consisting mainly of cows, chickens, cockerels, pigs and of course, his trusty working horse, Trampo.

Chapter Two

The Amazing Dragon Hatches

Just a few days after he brought the egg home, it hatched. Miller was not altogether surprised when a green dragon emerged, it was as if he'd been expecting one. What he didn't know was the moment he touched the egg the dragon got implanted into his mind. It's one of the mystical powers of dragon's eggs. He was, however, amazed, to see that the dragon had *three* heads. He took it out into the large barn, suspecting the baby dragon would not live through the night, but for some reason he couldn't explain, he felt it should be given every chance to survive. So he stayed up all night, keeping the little green dragon warm and regularly fed each of the mouths some raw eggs, mixed with a little milk he got from one of his cows.

The following morning, even though he was very tired, Miller knew that he'd have to push himself to get all his work done, and the little dragon would have to fend for itself. He left the dragon some eggs which he cracked into a bowl, and milked two of the cows and filled up a bucket, so the milk would last all day. He opened the door of the barn and stepped outside, but when he turned to close the door, he didn't see the invisible figure which stealthily slipped inside.

Miller then proceeded to the house and cooked himself a breakfast, ate it and went off to work.

During that first day, the three-headed dragon learnt how to walk. Unseen eyes watched in fascination as the little green dragon stumbled and fell many times, but it kept persevering and eventually, it managed to balance on its two rear legs and got steadier with each attempt. After eating some eggs and drinking lots of milk, the dragon seemed to be stronger and his attempts at walking grew easier.

The invisible observer was having strong fatherly feelings towards the dragon and he fought to resist them. He could not break the vow he made to himself, three hundred years ago, when he'd promised not to interfere with others' lives. Despite his efforts, his temptation to help the dragon grew stronger with each passing minute and he decided to leave the barn as quickly as he could. Leaving the little dragon alone, he dashed out and ran away from the farm.

Miller spent the day harvesting the wheat field, which he had planted eight months earlier. It took Trampo several trips, pulling the wagon back and forth between the field and the mill. At the end of each trip, Miller would unload the contents of the wagon into the grain store.

Trampo was an eighteen hands high, heavily built chestnut cob mare with a long, flowing almost-white mane and tail, both braided and knotted to keep them clean and out of the way when she was working. Like man, all the farm animals had been given the gift of long lives.

Even so, she was happy. Miller looked after her very well, feeding her the best oats and hay, renewing her bedding every morning and she was carefully groomed at the end of each working day. Miller shod her with new shoes whenever she needed them, and she had one day off a week to relax in the field, enjoying the blades of new grass to nibble and fresh sweet water to drink.

***

At the end of the day, he was surprised and glad to see the little dragon walking around the barn. All of the eggs had been eaten and the bucket of milk was empty.

"You have got on very well today, I will get some more eggs and milk for you," Miller said. He collected some eggs from the store and put them on the floor ready for the dragon, before going to milk one of the cows.

On seeing the eggs, the dragon scurried over to them. He reached out with his right arm and picked up an egg with his claws, then the claws on the other hand took the top off the egg and poured the contents into one of his mouths. The empty shell was carefully placed back onto the plate and each head was fed in turn the same way.

Miller glanced over in surprise and exclaimed. "How clever you are, feeding yourself in that way!" He continued to milk the cow and when he was finished, he put the bucket of milk on the floor. The dragon walked across to the bucket and started to drink, using each head in turn. Miller looked on, amazed. "It's so good that each head gets to taste the milk." He yawned loudly. "I'm sorry, but I have to leave you now "Good night."

Miller had a light supper of cheese and onions, with some bread and butter, and a small tankard of beer to wash it down. Halfway through his meal, he nodded off to sleep and woke up with a start when the tankard crashed to the floor. Exhausted, he drew himself up out of the chair and went to bed.

The following morning after breakfast, Miller prepared some eggs and milk for the dragon and set off to work. He was still tired because his working days were even longer now he was looking after the green dragon.

He collected the wheat grain from the mill store room and struggled through the day, grinding it down to flour. The large sacks he filled with the flour seemed to get heavier and heavier; it took every ounce of his strength to get the last one into the dry flour store.

When he finished working, he was keen to check on the dragon and see how it had progressed. Walking into the barn, he called out. "Are you getting along okay?" He was pleased to see the little dragon was still alive and seemed healthy, so he quickly collected some eggs and refilled the bucket of milk.

Once the dragon started eating the eggs, Miller walked towards the door of the barn. "I am very tired, I will see you in the morning. Good night."

The green dragon was so focused on eating, he didn't notice that Miller was leaving until the barn door closed with a soft bang. Three heads turned to look at the door before they glanced at one another. Then he carried on eating the eggs and drank the milk until it was all gone. Before it got too dark, the green dragon scurried over to a corner of the barn and slid down onto the floor, quickly falling fast asleep.

Chapter Three
The Dragon's First Weeks

Miller found his normal work routine had to change; he got up earlier each morning and went to bed later at night. He didn't mind having to do all this – he found he enjoyed looking after the dragon – but it was hard to make these changes. Working all those years, he had developed a natural rhythm between farming and the length of the days.

The Earth orbited around the sun on a different path and the Moon orbited Earth a little further away which meant the tides rose and fell less. The axis of Earth was vertical to the sun, not tilted over at an angle as it is today.

The farm provided for all his needs and the plentiful surplus from his requirements he used as barter. People visited on a regular basis to trade for the flour and corn, swapping tools or other useful items such as clothing and shoes. Several groups lived along the coast and only had fish, so they would come to trade with salted and smoked fish.

Wheat and maize were Miller's main crops in the fields, and in the kitchen garden, he grew lots of different vegetables including his favourite beans which he ate with his breakfast every morning. He would pick them fresh and cook them with his breakfast of eggs, bacon and bread. He also liked tomatoes, but for some unknown reason they would not grow on his land. Only occasionally did anyone bring them to barter and he would exchange almost anything to get them – even some of his precious beer.

There was always something to do. Once every ten days or so, Miller put a variety of vegetables from the kitchen garden into a large pot which was always kept over the fire for nine to ten days. It hung on a steel hook sited at the rear and just over the fire so it would keep the contents hot. Extra vegetables and water were added every few days, to keep the pot topped up. Most nights, Miller ate the stew with some bread for his supper.

Every week he baked a dozen loaves of bread, and every two weeks he made slabs of butter and cheese. At the end of each month, he made the beer that he liked to drink with his evening meal.

Miller had been looking after the green dragon for a week. The young one was growing fast on the milk and eggs. Each day Miller renewed the straw that the dragon used as a toilet. On the eighth day, he returned home from working in the fields, and found the dragon waiting just outside the barn.

"What are you up to?" he asked. Three heads turned around, the dragon looking into the barn without needing to move his body, which, Miller thought, was a useful thing to be able to do. He wished he could manage such a feat.

He walked into the barn and discovered several bales of hay stacked to make steps which allowed the dragon to climb up and open the door, and the eggs and milk were already prepared.

"Well, that is clever, using those hay bales like that and you milked the cow and gathered the eggs from the chickens! It is a big help to me if I don't need to prepare your food. It means I can just pop in to check that you are okay and get straight onto my work each morning. I can spend a little time with you at the end of each day."

Four days later, the dragon came up to the house while Miller was cooking his breakfast. Seeing the dragon by the door he said, "Good morning, come in, are you missing me that much? Or do you want some of my breakfast?"

The dragon walked inside, all three heads nodding in response.

Miller laughed. "Okay, I will give you something different to eat. I wondered when you would need something more substantial. Milk and eggs are probably not enough for a growing dragon."

The dragon still only came up to Miller's knee and could not reach the table, so Miller placed a chair at the end of the table, before he walked over to the dragon.

"Do not worry, I'm going to pick you up and put you on the chair so you can eat at the table with me." He gently picked up the green dragon and put him on the chair, before he proceeded to put some of the cooked beans, eggs and bacon on a wooden plate with a thick slice of bread, and placed it on the table in front of the dragon along with a spoon. Miller thought it would be easier to use. The dragon did nothing until Miller sat down and began to eat his breakfast with a knife and fork. The three heads with their six eyes watched Miller for a short while, before the dragon picked up the spoon and copied him, eating from the full plate with each head in turn.

"Would you like some beer?" Miller gave them a tankard half full of beer and said, "Drink it very slowly."

Each little head took it in turn to sip the beer.

Chapter Four
The New Cook

For six days, the green dragon appeared each morning to share breakfast with Miller. On the seventh day, Miller was awoken by clattering and banging coming from downstairs. Smelling food cooking, he smiled to himself and eagerly got dressed.

On entering the kitchen, he found the table set and two plates filled with food in place. The three-headed dragon was standing on one of the chairs and when he saw Miller, he placed a fried egg onto one of the plates. The kitchen was a mess, and some egg shells had fallen onto the floor, but Miller could not scold the dragon for trying so hard.

"You did this from just watching me?" Miller questioned. "Well done, this is a real treat! Would you like to do the cooking every morning?" All three heads nodded enthusiastically, and from that day on, the dragon cooked breakfast every morning. The dragon would start cooking early, so Miller could enjoy a little bit of extra rest. All three little heads nodded to one another when the idea was first thought of, because it was a kind thing to do for Miller as he worked very hard.

And so, the green dragon quickly became a good cook and housekeeper for Miller, while he busied himself working in either the fields or the mill from morning until night.

The dragon proved himself to be a quick learner, and only had to see how a task was done once before he knew how to carry it out skilfully himself, and he was always looking for new skills to learn. As Miller spent more and more time with the little dragon, he realized that each of the heads had a different personality. When he looked at the little dragon, he realized not one of the heads were identical and as time passed, he named them. Blue got his name because he had bright blue eyes and when he was younger, he often cried a lot. Blue could be recognized because he had one pointed peak on his head, and his was the head on the right when Miller looked at him.

The dragon's left head was named 'Sunny' by Miller. He named this head because Sunny was always happy and laughed a lot, and he had yellow eyes. They reminded Miller of the sunshine on a bright day. Sunny had two pointed peaks on his head.

The third head, the one in the centre, had red eyes, and three peaks upon his head. After giving Sunny and Blue their names, the third little dragon head had looked up at Miller and stared at him. Miller had laughed, and said, "Why, I have no name to give you right now!" And from that day on the third little dragon head was referred to as 'No-Name' and before long, the name had stuck.

Miller would eventually teach the three-headed dragon every job on the farm, starting with feeding the chickens. The first time the dragon fed the chickens, Sunny popped some chicken feed into his mouth, but he spat it out very quickly, it felt like grit against Sunny's tongue and it had no taste. Sunny could not understand why the chickens clucked and scratched around so eagerly, to eat the horrible stuff.

The three cows had names one was called Dark Eyes because she had a black spot over each eye; the second was called One Spot because she had only one large black spot on her side. The third cow was totally white so she was called Whitehide and all three cows spent every day outside, grazing in the fields around the farm. At the end of each day, they had to be rounded up and brought into the barn for milking and bedding down for the night. Milking them was one of the dragon's favourite jobs, the milk tasted so good straight from the cows and it was still warm. The dragon had lots of fun trying to catch the milk in each of his mouths; as it was squirted in the air, the milk tended to go everywhere – in his eyes, up his nostrils and even in his ears.

Cleaning out the barn at the end of the day was no fun at all to begin with, not until the green dragon started to roll around in the fresh, new hay. Miller told the dragon that he resembled the pigs, who loved rolling in the mud. Sunny, No-Name and Blue tried playing hide and seek too, with two heads hiding beneath the hay, but the third head knew exactly where they were, so that was no fun at all.

Several weeks went by and one day Miller was joined by the dragon out in the field. He was with Trampo ploughing and preparing the soil to plant seeds of wheat.

There were no seasons in the old world, so planting was carried out once a crop had been harvested. The dragon watched how the job was done and was soon helping. By the time the green dragon was two years old, each of the heads could talk for themselves, and had grown to just above Miller's waist. They were happy living together and Miller's life had become much easier.

Whenever people came to barter for Miller's goods, they would stay for a while to talk with Miller and the dragon. One day, a couple who Miller had never met before came to barter for some flour and corn. Miller was shocked into silence at the resemblance he could see between them and his parents. For a few moments, he was stunned, but he quickly came back to his senses when the man spoke to him about his requirements.

In bed that night, memories of his parent's deaths came flooding back. He realised then that since he found the dragons egg, he had not dwelt on the loss of his parents. Now he remembered vividly what had happened all those years ago, he had thought at the time that they were unlucky, but now he understood the meaning of fate.

Both of his parents had been killed in a terrible landslide, in an area of the mountains where they visited regularly. If they had not gone that day, Miller knew they would have lived for many more years. The accident happened just before his parents turned one hundred and forty-two years old, still quite young.

Miller had been inside the farmhouse when he heard the terrible roar of the mountain.

He'd run all the way from the farmhouse, but by the time he got there the landslide had stopped and he could see that half the mountain had collapsed. Despite believing there was little hope, he still spent the day frantically searching in different locations in hopes of finding them.

By night fall he was exhausted, and he slumped down onto the ground, certain that his parents were gone. There was nothing more he could do, so he decided to go home, thinking that the mountain was a fitting resting place for them, because it was a place where they had loved to visit.

Miller pushed the sad memories aside and decided to focus on his life with his new little friend. The green dragon's arrival had changed his life for the better, and he was happy to spend his time with Sunny, Blue and No-Name.

***

Miller and the dragon lived and worked, side-by-side for over twenty years. During that time, Miller found himself deeply contented with the dragon's company. Talking to No-Name, Blue, and Sunny meant he was never lonely and the days seemed to pass by very quickly. They were constant companions, and Miller particularly enjoyed their meal times together, which would often last for several hours with plenty of things to talk about. In all that time together, Miller never thought to tell No-Name, Sunny and Blue that they were a dragon. It just never seemed that important to point it out. No-Name, Sunny and Blue were his friends and that was all that mattered.

The heads had never questioned who they were or how they came to be living with Miller, and as the years passed, the dragon grew to be more than twice as tall as Miller.

One morning, the dragon came inside to make breakfast and found Miller slumped in his chair. He had fallen asleep and died peacefully during the night, just a few weeks after his one hundred and ninetieth birthday.

No-Name, Sunny and Blue were devastated by Miller's death and the three heads all cried for a long time together. When they had cried themselves out, No-Name suggested that they should bury Miller on the same mountain where his parents had died so many years before.

Chapter Five

The Growing Dragon

Over the next ten years, the green dragon continued to grow, living off the farm's produce, very much the same way as Miller had. The green dragon had not only grown taller and longer, but his green-spotted tummy had gotten bigger with each passing year, until now, when it was lumpy and round and dragged along the ground. While Miller had remained slim with all the hard work he did each day, the green dragon just got fatter and fatter. On the end of his large, lumpy bumpy tail he had a big set of spikes which made a strange bang, thumping sound whenever he walked.

Smooth, shield-shaped scales covered the sides and upper part of his body and these continued over each neck and head, the scales somewhat distorted due to the large amount of bulk they had to cover. His two large rear legs had large feet, each sporting four long toes and short sharp claws. Three of the claws faced the front and one pointed towards the rear. They made a lot of noise when the three-headed dragon was walking. The dragon's two small arms had five fingers each, all with very sharp claws. They were very dexterous and useful for all the work and cooking he had to do. The dragon didn't know how to fly, even though he had large, rubbery, bat-like wings that were folded away into slits along its sides. Triangular, flexible shaped peaks ran along each neck and down his body and the tail.

Eventually, the green dragon grew so big, he knew it wouldn't be long before he wouldn't be able to get into the house to cook. No-Name, Sunny and Blue discussed the problem for quite some time, and decided the best thing to do would be to move the kitchen equipment out into the barn. It was no easy task, because the cooking range needed to be dismantled and rebuilt, and a new chimney would have to be constructed against one of the barn's walls. The green dragon collected all the stones he would need from around the farm's fields. Trampo patiently pulled the cart along, while the green dragon loaded the cart full of stones and then unloaded them into the barn.

Green Three Headed Dragon

Meanwhile, that same invisible watcher was keeping an eye on No-Name, Blue and Sunny. In all the years that the dragon had lived on Miller's farm, the invisible watcher had continued to watch the dragon's activities with a great deal of interest. Checking up on the three-headed dragon, he slipped into the barn to watch the construction of the chimney. For reasons he couldn't explain, he was drawn to the green dragon, and as time passed felt compelled to be near him.

The first attempt to build the chimney was a disaster; No-Name, Sunny and Blue had managed to build almost half the chimney, but because it was leaning alarmingly towards one side, it all fell down. One large stone landed on one of the dragon's toes, and all three heads cried out together in pain.

The invisible watcher had been viewing the dragon's building efforts, and he had to slip out of the barn quickly, stifling his laughter. Seeing the dragon hopping about on one foot had been so funny, he couldn't contain himself. He slipped away, vowing to come back again soon.

No-Name had thought that the best way to build the chimney was to copy the one in the house. Determined not to make the same mistake a second time, No-Name devised a simple way to ensure the chimney was straight, by using a length of string with a small stone tied at one end. They used mud to bond the stones together as they built the chimney steadily upwards. It took several more days to complete, and when it was finally finished, Sunny and Blue nodded and smiled saying together, "What a good job we've done! Miller would have been proud of us."

The first meal they cooked on the new range seemed tastier than anything they had cooked before, and No-Name suggested it was because the work they had done had been so exhausting, the food tasted better as a reward for their hard work. The barn had always been cold and damp in the mornings especially if it had rained during the night, but now the fire would keep the barn warm and cosy.

Chapter Six

A New Family

Two days later, the green dragon was tidying up after breakfast and preparing to leave the barn to start work in the fields, when sounds of voices talking and the neighing of a horse could be heard from outside. He went to investigate and saw some small people standing around a wagon which had pulled up outside the old farmhouse. It's sides were brightly painted with colourful flowers and a wonderful sun burst.

No-Name whispered to Blue and Sunny. "These little people are human children," he said, hoping not to startle them. In a louder voice, he spoke to the children. "Hello little ones. Don't be afraid, we are very friendly."

None of the children showed any fear, because they had heard about the friendly, three-headed dragon who lived at the farm. All five of them came running towards the green dragon and started to sing and skip. After a few seconds of watching them, the green dragon joined in the fun. Although it was something the dragon had never done before, it just seemed so natural.

The children's parents watched on in amazement, they could hardly believe the sight before their eyes and started clapping their hands to the sound of the children and the dragon singing 'Ring Around the Roses'. When the children fell to the ground at the end of the song, they were even more delighted when the green dragon fell down too. They all rolled around on the ground chattering and giggling, and after a while, the dragon, still somewhat out of breath, struggled back onto his feet.

Sunny was the first to introduce himself

"Hello, I am Sunny." Sunny nodded to the children, offering them a cheerful smile.

"Hi, I am Blue," Blue said. He inclined his head towards No-Name. "This is No-Name."

Beginning the dance again, the children introduced themselves, calling out their names in turn.

"Hi I'm Susan," the first girl said. She was slim and tall, with long blonde hair and beautiful blue eyes. "I'm fourteen, and I'm the oldest."

A young boy spoke next. "I'm Mark and I'm twelve." Even though he was two years younger he was almost the same height as Susan, and had blonde hair and brown eyes.

"Hi, I'm Tank and I'm ten." The green dragon noticed that Tank was a lot shorter and stockier, with straight brown hair and brown eyes.

"I'm Tim and I am nine," said the third little boy. He had blonde hair and blue eyes, and he put his arm around a smaller girl standing beside him. He continued "This is Tame, she's my twin sister and she is very shy." Tame resembled a pretty doll, with wavy blonde hair, eyes of blue and the whitest skin the green dragon had ever seen on a human. He thought she looked like her mother.

The children's parents came closer to the dragon and the man introduced himself politely. "Hello, my name is Stage. I'm glad to meet you. We've heard a lot about you and couldn't wait to meet you." Stage stood very straight and had broad shoulders with muscular arms and a developed six-pack could be seen under his tight fitting shirt. His short black hair curled close to his scalp defining his sharp features, his dark brown eyes were nearly black. The green dragon could see that he was a proud, strong and healthy man. "This is my wife, Act."

Act was shorter than her husband, and her middle was rounded, but her legs were slim and her arms were muscular. Her wavy blonde hair hung halfway down her back, she stood erect as proud as her husband.

"It's hard to believe we have lived here for thirty years, and your children are the first we have ever met," Sunny and Blue then said, speaking together as they were often prone to doing. "This has been such a special time. We've never had so much fun before! You have delightful, friendly, and happy children."

Stage smiled. "Thank you. It hasn't been easy bringing them up these past few years. Since we lost our farm in a fire two years ago, we've been forced to return to our old trade, working as travelling performers, but we spend weeks at a time travelling around searching for groups of people to entertain. When it was just the two of us, it didn't matter, but our children deserve a much better life.

The three-headed dragon was sympathetic to Stage's story. Sunny, Blue and No-Name glanced at one another, before No-Name spoke. "Would you put on a show for us?"

Act replied instantly. "We would love to, but it would take a while for us to get prepared."

"That would be wonderful," Blue responded. "We have work to do on the farm and will not be back until the evening. Could you stay until then?"

"Of course we can," Stage agreed with a broad smile.

"If you place your wagon under the lean-to by the barn, you can unhitch your horse and take him around the back; there are separate stables which you can use. He can keep our horse, Trampo, company," No-Name said.

Stage thanked them and guided his large black cob stallion under the lean-to, before unhitching him from the wagon. The horse stood tall and proud, with white flashes covering his four hooves, and a distinctive white star on his forehead.

"That's a fine-looking horse you have there – what's his name?" Sunny and Blue asked together.

"We call him White Star." The children stopped dancing and gathered around their father, they wanted to help with White Star and announced they were excited to meet Trampo.

The three-headed dragon walked away heading out to the fields, before No-Name turned back and spoke again. "You can draw some water from the well to give White Star, it's located just behind the barn. Please use the farmhouse if you wish to prepare some food, or sit and relax." And with that, the green dragon stomped off to begin the day's work.

Working in the fields, Sunny, Blue and No-Name discussed Stage and Act's difficult life.

"I'd like to help this family," No-Name said, "But we need to be careful how we go about it. I have an idea. Why don't we ask them if they would stay and help us on the farm for a few weeks, then later, we could invite them to stay on permanently?"

"What a marvellous idea," Blue and Sunny said, with a firm nod of their heads.

At the end of the day the green dragon came back to the farmhouse. Stage was standing just outside the door and looked up at the sun setting with a worried expression on his face. "I'm very sorry, it's going to get dark soon, and we need the sunlight to perform."

No-Name glanced at Sunny and Blue, and smiled widely. This was a perfect way of getting the family to stay for a little longer. "That's no problem at all! If you don't mind staying until tomorrow, we can take some time off then to watch you perform."

Stage exchanged a glance with Act, and the three-headed dragon saw Act smile and nod her agreement. "We rarely stop in one place for long, but it's such a lovely farm, we would love to stay on."

The children all began to jump up and down excitedly, looking very pleased with the idea of staying.

"That sounds good to us," Sunny and Blue said. "And as payment for your performance, we will provide and cook breakfast for everyone in the morning."

Tank rubbed his belly in excitement, but

then, because he was a little unsure what might be on the menu he asked tentatively, "Please, what will you be cooking?"

Happy to see that Tank was so enthusiastic about breakfast, No-Name responded. "Fresh beans from the vegetable garden, eggs and bacon, and some home-baked bread. How does that sound?"

Stage and Act both looked delighted.

"Yummy, that sounds great!" Tank announced happily.

Susan piped up. "We have lots of fresh tomatoes; we grow them in pots in the back of the wagon because we love them so much. Would you cook some of them for breakfast as well?"

The three-headed dragon was so excited, he began bouncing up and down on the spot, his big spotted belly wobbled up and down. Sunny and Blue replied "Of course! We like them so much, but for some reason, they won't grow on the farm."

***

Coincidentally, the following day would be the dragon's thirtieth birthday and No-Name, Sunny and Blue could think of no better way to spend it than with Stage and Act and their five lovely children.

Sunny and Blue had been passing thoughts back and forth to one another, thinking about what they could give No-Name as a birthday gift. When Miller was alive, he'd always celebrated their birthday with much excitement and celebration, and would make each of the heads a separate gift. One year, he'd given each of them a necklace with a sparkly stone in the centre of it, the stones chosen to match the colour of their eyes. Another year, Miller had given them a stone which they could use to file their talons when they got split or broken. The funniest gift he'd given them were matching straw hats, to help keep the sun off their heads.

They looked back on those birthdays with very fond memories, and Sunny and Blue decided the best gift of all for No-Name would be to help find him a name of his own.

Chapter Seven

A Birthday Surprise

Early the following morning, the green dragon started to prepare breakfast, he collected eggs from the chickens, picked a basket full of sweet, crunchy beans from the vegetable garden, and sliced bacon ready to put in the frying pan.

A few minutes after they'd arrived in the barn, Susan came in, with a basket full of ripe, red tomatoes.

"Where shall I put these?" she asked.

The three-headed dragon clasped his hands together in delight. "They look absolutely delicious! Please put them on the table," No-Name requested.

Stage entered the barn to ask if he could help.

"Could you set up a trestle table outside, so we can all eat together?" Sunny asked.

"Yes, I can do that. We'll perform for you after breakfast and then, reluctantly, we'll need to be on our way" replied Stage.

No-Name, Sunny and Blue glanced at one another, but remained silent.

When breakfast was ready, several of the older children came to the barn door and offered to carry the food outside.

"Thank you," Blue announced, thinking what lovely children they were. Within minutes, the children had carefully carried the food outside and filled the table.

Once all the food had been served, the green dragon appeared and stood at the end of the table, and smiled broadly at the family, who were gathered around the table. "Breakfast is served," No-Name announced.

An argument started between the children, who all wanted to be the one who got to sit next to the three-headed dragon.

Stage spoke firmly to his five children. "I think it would be a good idea if the youngest children sit closest to No-Name, Blue and Sunny." The children agreed and quickly took their positions at the table.

Sunny and Blue glanced at each other and cleared their throats very loudly, startling No-Name and everyone else at the table.

"Before we start eating breakfast, we have something important to say," Sunny announced. "Blue and I would like to wish No-Name a very happy thirtieth birthday!"

"It's your birthday?" Susan asked, clapping her hands. "Happy Birthday!"

"Happy birthday, No-Name!" Stage, Act and all the children shouted together. "And happy birthday to Blue and Sunny, too!"

Sunny grinned and spoke again, turning to face No-Name. "Blue and I wanted to give you a special present, No-Name. Miller never thought of a special name for you before he died, but we'd like to help you now, to find a name that is perfect for you."

No-Name's eyes were wide as he stared at first Blue, then Sunny. "I'm… I'm…" Tears filled No-Name's eyes. "Thank you, thank you so much. What a wonderful surprise! You were very clever, to keep this surprise from me!"

"Not really," Blue said, as he shook his head. "You know that Sunny and I have always been able to converse mind-to-mind with one another – we just made sure to keep it from you!"

Everyone spent a few minutes talking about Sunny and Blue's surprise for No-Name, and tucked in to their delicious breakfast.

When the three-headed dragon had finished eating, Sunny turned to Stage and asked. "Do you remember when you said you've spent a lot of your time travelling around from place to place, and you didn't think it was any good for the children?"

Stage glanced at Act before he answered simply. "Yes, I do. We've enjoyed staying here very much, and the children have loved being here."

Blue and Sunny looked at one another, before turning their attention back to Stage. "Would you mind staying on and looking after the farm, so we could leave and help No-Name to find a name of his own?"

Stage glanced at his children who were all nodding their heads enthusiastically, then he turned to Act and asked her. "What do you think? I think we should do it."

Act was beaming, and nodded excitedly "Yes, it would be wonderful! How long do you think you will be away?" she asked, looking to the green dragon for an answer.

No-Name spoke, and shook his head. While Blue and Sunny had obviously been planning behind his back, he'd had no idea they intended to leave the farm. "I'm very happy for you to stay on here at the farm, but I'm not sure we can burden you with this."

"Nonsense," Stage said. "You are giving us somewhere to live, a chance for our children to settle somewhere and be happy. You can go for as long as it takes you to discover a name, and we will gladly stay until you return."

For a moment, No-Name seemed to be thinking about arguing, but then he nodded his head, tears filled his eyes. "Thank you, so very much."

Once breakfast was finished Stage stood up. "That was indeed a feast, we have never eaten so much delicious food!" He took up his tankard of beer and turned to the green dragon. "To the most gracious of hosts and the best cooks we have ever met. We salute you and thank you for your hospitality and friendship. Go out into Pangreat and know that we will keep the farm running for you. We sincerely hope you find what you are looking for "Cheers!"

"Cheers!" the children shouted, drinking from their tankards of fresh, creamy milk.

"That was very kind of you, and I must thank you again for your generosity in carrying out this enormous favour," No-Name responded.

The green dragon got onto his feet. "Shall we be off now?" Blue enquired.

Sunny laughed. "Yes, let's get started on this adventure immediately!" Three heads quickly turned this way and that, they waved and shouted goodbye to Stage, Act and their five lovely children, before he began walking along the path leading to the fields. The quest had begun!

The invisible watcher stood in the shadows of a nearby cornfield, watching the scene before him intently. He had heard everything that transpired and was happy to see this family helping out the three-headed dragon, and being rewarded in return.

He made a swift decision to follow the dragon on its quest.

"Perhaps then, I might find out why I am so drawn to this three-headed dragon."

Chapter Eight

The Grimy Giant

The green dragon walked along the track that took him out past the furthest farm fields away from the farmhouse. So far, none of the heads had given much thought to exactly where they were going. Now as the dragon walked along, he started to make quite a lot of noise, with the *thump, thump, thump* of his big heavy strides and the *bong, bong, bong* of his large tail hitting the ground. And of course, being a dragon, there was much burping and farting, which created quite a din.

An hour later No-Name turned to look at Sunny and Blue. "I think we need to stop and think about which way we're going, otherwise we might get lost, or even end up back where we've started from, before we've finished our quest. I believe the best way to do this, is to try and keep walking in as straight a line as possible and head towards some prominent land mark in the distance." No-Name glanced around, but for as far as the eye could see, the land in front of them remained flat.

Sunny pointed towards the horizon. "Can you see that flat-topped mountain? Perhaps that would do."

No-Name's red eyes twinkled with excitement. "How did you spot that so quickly? This is one of the advantages of having three sets of eyes! Let's get going."   None of the heads had any idea of how far away the flat-topped mountain was, or how long it would take them to walk there.

The terrain appeared to be flat, but they soon discovered that shrubs were growing everywhere and they hid lots of rocks which were difficult to see, so the green dragon had to walk slowly and carefully to avoid falling over. It took him nearly a week to reach the flat-topped mountain which as they drew closer, seemed to have a bow right across the top forming a small valley.

They stopped and stared up at it for a while, before they decided to follow the winding river that flowed from a hidden source somewhere from the base of the steep cliff.
The slow flowing river twisted and meandered for several miles until they came across a large wooden house, that was massive in comparison to their barn.

Just outside the house was a giant, sitting down on a large stool. When he saw them coming he stood up, he was at least three times taller than the green dragon. No-Name, Blue and Sunny discovered they only reached the top of his legs.

The giant wore only a loin cloth, his dirty arms and legs were bare and covered in, curly black hair. The green dragon noticed that even the giant's large hands were ingrained with dirt and his fingernails were full of black muck. It looked as if the giant had been using his hands to dig up roots.

On his enormous feet, the giant wore what appeared to be lumps of tree trunk, tied into place with heavy leather straps.

His bumpy, bald head appeared to have been bashed a few times, with lumps and bumps and scars all over the place. Small tufts of straggly grey hair dotted his scalp, and seemed to be growing out of both his nostrils and his ears. He had only a few teeth in his large, offset mouth and they resembled black fangs.

One green eye seemed to follow the green-dragon as he walked, while the other eye stared off in a different direction, as if it was looking at something to the side of the dragon. It appeared he had never taken a bath or even had a wash, and his smelly body stunk of rotten eggs and boiled cabbage.

Not someone to spend too much time with, No-Name thought to himself.

Rock the Giant

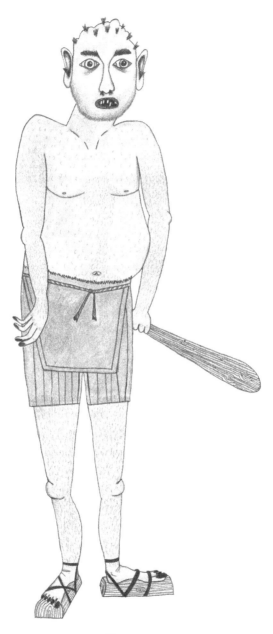

Sunny was the first to speak. "Good morning."

"Is it?" replied the giant.

"Of course it is. What's your name?" Sunny asked.

"Rock," said the giant. "What's yours?".

"My name is Sunny"

"Hello, my name is Blue." Blue added, as he watched the giant quite nervously.

No-Name spoke next. "I haven't got a name, that's why we're travelling along this path. We're on a quest to find me a name.

"Do you live here alone?" Blue asked curiously.

Rock replied in a deep, gruff voice. "No, I live here with my wife but she's away for a few days, helping the children."

Sunny and Blue were rather surprised by his answer, but decided that even though he was smelly and dirty, there was no reason why the giant shouldn't have a wife and children. "Do you have any ideas for a good name?"

Rock was silent for a moment or two, rubbing the top of his head with his dirty hand before he announced some very strange names, but the three-headed dragon didn't think any of them would suit No-Name.

Rock glanced up at the sun and squinted. "It looks as if it's just past midday. Would you like something to eat?"

Sunny shook his head and Blue responded for all three of them. "No, thank you, we haven't got the time. We must hurry off and continue our quest."

The three-headed dragon couldn't wait to get away from the terrible pong, and shuffled off as quickly as he could.

After a while they slowed down and discussed their quest. All three heads admitted to experiencing strong feelings of urgency.

"I feel guilty about leaving the family to work on our farm," No-Name said. "I believe that's the main reason I feel so impatient and can't wait to get on with the quest.

Sunny and Blue agreed "We must try and get back to them as fast as we can. Each morning we should start as soon as it gets light. We need to walk quickly and not take too many breaks. If we keep going until it gets dark every day we should cover more ground."

The invisible watcher smiled to himself, pleased when he heard the dragon admit to suffering guilty feelings about leaving the farm with the family. He was realising just how thoughtful they were; a character trait he had rarely observed in his lifetime.

Chapter Nine

The Grumpy Tuskun

The three-headed dragon stopped and looked around for another prominent feature to head towards.

"What about those three peaks?" Blue and Sunny suggested.

No-Name replied immediately. "We live just by those peaks." No-Name searched the horizon in the opposite direction.

"Look there," Sunny suggested. "That mountain resembles the giant's big toe and it's in the right direction. It seems about the same distance as we've just travelled, so I think we should go that way." They set off at a faster pace, the ground was getting clearer, so they could make better time.

Four days later, they were in sight of the giant's toe mountain. Halfway up the mountain, silver light could be seen streaming out of a crevice. Further down, it was joined by several other slithers of silver, all of them flowing together, and the three-headed dragon realized it was one large stream of water, twinkling beneath the sunlight. The torrent of white foam and froth tumbled down over the rocks below. It flowed down the mountain in a long, straight line, until it reached a void and developed into a wide beautiful, cascading waterfall. It smashed down onto the rocks below with so much force, it sounded like thunder.

A large pool had formed at the base of the waterfall and where the sun shone over the surface, it reflected like diamonds. Where the water splashed down over the rocks, a large colourful rainbow formed, something they had never seen before. They stood watching it in awe, before it gradually faded away. Lots of fish could be seen splashing and swimming in the shallows and No-Name, Sunny and Blue all agreed it was very beautiful.

Before they moved on, a large Tuskun walked out from behind the torrent of water. The three-headed dragon suspected he must have been hiding back there. The Tuskun shook itself violently, splashed water everywhere, before he went down on all fours and rushed quickly towards them. He went closer and closer and stopped abruptly just in front of the dragon and rocked back onto his rear legs and stretched up to his full height. He stared up at them fearlessly through small, pig-like eyes, as his gaze darted frantically from one of the dragon's heads to the next in confusion.

The Tuskun snarled, and opened its large mouth to reveal sharp white teeth, and No-Name, Sunny and Blue could smell raw fish on the Tuskun's breath. Two long tusks grew from either side of his lower jaw, pushing aside the thick brown lips, and the tusks grew up over the sides of the face, framing the piggy-like nose and eyes. The tusks continued up past the Tuskun's pointed ears and curled over the top of its small head. The green dragon thought they resembled an antelope's horns.

Thick, dank wet fur, which seemed to have slimy green pieces of material interwoven into it, covered the Tuskun's body. Except for the feet and hands, which were big and hairless, and the toes, long and skinny with small talons for nails. The hands were similar, but the Tuskun had large, chunky knuckles, obviously because he used them to walk on. These extra-long arms helped him move very fast and the three-headed dragon imagined he would be a good rock and tree climber.

As the three-headed dragon stared at him, he started to scratch his own head in puzzlement.

"Hello, how are you?" No-Name announced after a few minutes had passed.

The Tuskun answered nervously, in a voice which sounded more like a growl. "I am fine."

"That's good to hear. And what's your name?" No-Name questioned.

"Grath. What's yours?" the Tuscan snarled.

Grath The Grumpy Tuscan

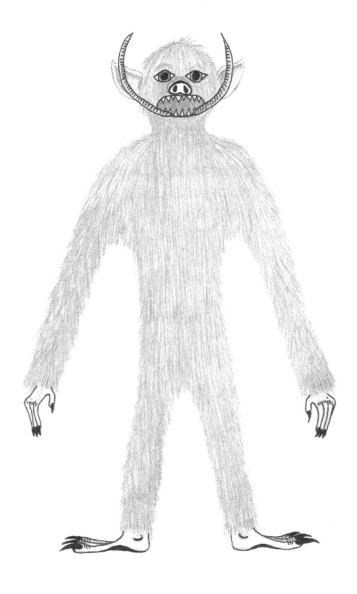

No-Name shook his head. "I haven't got one, but this is Sunny, and he's Blue," he said, nodding towards each of the heads in turn. "Do you live here alone? It's such a lovely place."

"Yes, we male Tuscans always live on our own, until we find a mate. I live in a cave behind the waterfall," Grath explained gruffly.

"May we look inside?" Sunny and Blue asked curiously.

Grath replied reluctantly. "Yes, you can, but don't go stomping around inside."

Together, the three heads stretched their necks through the curtain of water for a quick look inside. All three shuddered, not only because of the freezing cold water, but also at the sight which greeted their eyes. The cave behind the waterfall smelled damp, just like wet, smelly socks. Green slippery moss could be seen covering every visible surface and it looked snotty and slimy and disgusting.

The three heads had seen enough and pulled their heads out rather quickly, glad to be in the fresh air again. "Are you comfortable in there?" No-Name asked politely.

Grath stared at him suspiciously. "Yes, I am, it's a palace."

No-Name changed the subject quickly, not wanting to offend the Tuscan. "We are on a quest to find me a name. Do you have any good ideas?"

The Tuscan thought for a moment or two, pursing his thick brown lips. "What about Try or Triple, if you are the third head," said Grath.

"Try sounds really good; what do you both think?" No-Name asked, looking at the other two. Neither of them said anything, instead staring down at the ground.

"Well it does sound a bit like me, I like to *try* different things," No-Name said.

"Something about it, is not quite right," Sunny and Blue announced together.

"What about Triple?" No-Name asked.

"You weren't born third, I popped my head out last," Blue said. "If you had been the third born, then it would be a good and suitable name for you, but you weren't."

"So, that's not the right name either," Sunny added.

No-Name had to agree with them and he quickly dismissed both possibilities.

"It all sounds rather complicated to me!" Grath said rudely. "If I thought it was going to be like this, I would not have gotten involved. Go away! I have no time for all of this, I'm due to take my daily bath in the river." With that, he suddenly jumped in the river, ignored the dragon, and dived beneath the water.

The green dragon was left with nothing

more to do but move on. As they walked away Sunny and Blue spoke. "He was rather rude."

"I suspect he isn't very clever – did you notice he has a very small head in relation to the size of his body?" No-Name pointed out.

The invisible watcher smiled to himself, from his spot a little further back along the path. He thought that even though the three-headed dragon was now thirty years old, he was still very young and had a long way to go before he became fully grown, not only in stature, but also in adult thinking. His sheltered life on the farm had restricted his development and he still couldn't fly, but the invisible watcher was certain if the dragon kept going in the right direction, these issues would be resolved.

Chapter Ten

The Wise Old Oak Tree

"Where next, do you think?" No-Name asked.

Sunny had spotted somewhere already and he and Blue answered together. "That wooded mountain looks as if it's in the right direction, and it's not as far as the last walk."

"You're getting even better at this, because you're able to look in two places at once and think back and forth with each other," No-Name told them with a broad smile.

Three days later, the green dragon approached a dense, wooded area.

The invisible watcher had decided it would be best to stay well away from Oak-ley, who lived in the direction the green dragon had decided upon. He had met her before and didn't want her to sense his presence. He stopped following No-Name, Sunny and Blue, and found a place where he could hide and rest, but keep watch at the same time.

Just at the very edge of the forest, Sunny and Blue noticed what appeared to be an extremely old oak tree. The dragon slowed down as it walked by the tree, three heads turned together to stare at it, because they had never seen such an impressive tree before.

The tree began to creak and groan; it twisted around and watched the dragon as he walked by.

Hearing the strange sounds, the green dragon came to a stop. Sunny was first to speak, as he watched the tree curiously. "Okay, stop hiding in the tree and show yourself, please! We will not harm you, we are friendly."

Slowly, two large, twisted, gnarled and leafy branches unfurled, that revealed a face. Much to the green dragon's surprise, years of exposure to wind and rain hadn't affected the face at all. Its large eyes were clearly defined, as was a most noble little nose. Another noisy creak exposed a gently curved mouth, huge in comparison to the rest of the face. The tree spoke in a deep voice. "I am Oak-ley. How nice to meet you, at last!"

No-Name responded somewhat surprised. "Have you been expecting us?"

Oak-ley replied in her soft, rich voice. "Yes, I have."

"How could that be?" No-Name asked.

"I'm over one thousand, seven hundred and fifty years old and I've heard and seen many things during those years, including seeing a red one-headed dragon like yourselves."

Oakley the Old Oak Tree

No-Name interrupted abruptly. "What do you mean, by 'dragon'? I'm sorry, but we don't understand.

Oak-ley answered. "I have known of your existence since you were discovered under a bush. I was aware that you stayed with the man who brought you up and he did not tell you what you were. My dears, you are an exceptional dragon! I know you are still young, but surely you must have had some idea of what you are?"

Sunny and Blue stared at each other, having trouble understanding what Oak-ley had said. For once, the two of them were stuck for words. No-Name thought for a minute or two and turned to Blue and Sunny. All three spoke in unison. "We are a dragon!" Sharing an exuberant grin, No-Name turned back to Oak-ley. "Can you tell us if you have you seen the red dragon recently?"

"Yes," Oak-ley replied. "I have seen the red dragon flying overhead just a few weeks ago, and like most dragons, she can breathe fire!"

"How do you know so much, when you are rooted to one spot?" No-Name asked.

"You are right, I am stuck in the one spot, but my roots spread out in every direction and wherever they are touched by the roots of another plant or tree, thoughts and news are passed to me through these connections. It's how trees and plants talk to one another. Plus, my acorns have been spread far and wide by the birds and the animals, so I have offspring in many different places across the land, who in turn, have their acorns scattered. Oak trees grow in every corner of Pangreat, so the strongest thoughts come from them."

"That is amazing! How do you listen to all those voices at once?" Sunny and Blue asked.

"Listening to their thoughts is not the same as the way we are talking now. The stories and news I hear are in tree language, which is much simpler to understand, and I can shut them off when I'm tired of listening."

"That sounds even more complicated," No-Name announced.

Oak-ley shook her trunk, and the three-headed dragon was showered in a flurry of leaves. "It's not really," she reassured them with another broad smile, and changed the subject. "I will offer you one piece of advice. The farmer loved you, so do not think badly of him for not telling you what you were."

No-Name exchanged a glance with Sunny and Blue. "I don't think any of us thinks badly of him, we loved him, too," he announced.

"We agree, he was like a father to us," Sunny said. "Let us introduce ourselves; I'm Sunny."

Blue butted in. "I'm called Blue. We keep being surprised by the new people we meet, and it's great to meet you, too. Did you know our names before we arrived? And that we were on a quest to find a proper name for No-Name?"

"Yes," Oak-ley said. "I had heard about your quest, but not what your names were. There are so many names in the world, I stopped translating them from tree language over two hundred years ago."

"Oh! So, you couldn't help me to discover what my name is?" No-Name asked, sounding disappointed.

"No, I'm afraid not," Oak-ley replied. "You don't need my help, No-Name. It's my understanding that finding an appropriate name means that you must find it for yourself. Any names given to you by others will just complicate things and make your choice even harder. You will know instinctively which one is right."

No-Name nodded. "Yes, you are correct. I think I already knew that, but I didn't realise it until now. How wise you are! Can we stay and talk to you for a while? We would love to get to know you better."

"That would please me so very much," Oak-ley replied.

She was such good company, they stayed

and talked to her for most of the morning. Oak-ley told them about many of the different insects and birds which lived within her canopy. She was never alone; a fox lived under a root to her left and a badger and his family lived in a group of roots to the right. Her large hollow trunk provided a home to some bats and a hive of honey bees, and a red squirrel lived in a hole in one of her branches.

"Two fairies visit me a few times each year; they live with other fairies."

"Could you tell us where they live? We would love to visit them, too," No-Name asked.

Oak-ley was initially worried about how the fairies might react to meeting the dragon, but she knew that if the fairies were too afraid they would stay in hiding, so she told them. "Near the sea, by a large group of mountains which have five peaks that resemble a circle of stones. It's over in that direction. They are lovely singers and play a lot." Oak-ley pointed out the way with one of her branches.

"Thank you! We will come back another time to see you again," No-Name said.

"Goodbye!" Oak-ley said.

Sunny and Blue replied "Goodbye" As the green dragon walked off, he turned around and waved.

Oak-ley waved one of her huge branches.

"Don't forget, I will learn about whatever you discover; remember the trees talk to one another all the time."

***

During the three-headed dragon's visit with Oak-ley, the invisible watcher remained in his hiding place, observing them talking together. He was too far away to hear what they had said and had to admit, it was a strange sight to see the massive oak tree conversing with the green, three-headed dragon.

His thoughts turned back three hundred years, to the day when he'd discovered the invisible cloak.

He had been one hundred years old then, and nearly eight feet tall. Walking through some rather dense woods, he'd been ducking under a low branch when he felt something fall onto his left shoulder. Reaching up with his hand to brush it off, he had instinctively looked down to discover what had fallen on him. He was shocked and somewhat frightened to discover his shoulder had disappeared! Touching the space where his shoulder should be, he felt something with his right hand. He gripped it with his fingers and pulled it across his body, surprised when that too, began to disappear. How relieved he was, to discover that what had dropped down over his shoulder was an invisible cloak, with a large, loose hood. It fit him from head to toe, the hem brushed along the ground, and when he wore it, he was completely invisible!

Grambold believed the cloak was a gift, given to him so he could travel around the whole of Pangreat without being seen. Using the cloak, he could study whatever he came across during his travels, study it without his presence being known, and record whatever he learned. This, he concluded, was because as far as he was aware, he was the only human who could read and write, after he had been taught by his father.

Over time, Grambold discovered that the cloak could only be worn for short periods of time, because it sapped both his strength and energy and the older he got, the worse his energy was sapped. It was the main reason he stayed a long way behind the green dragon, relying on finding places to hide away, rather than always using the cloak.

Magically it kept him looking young he had hardly any wrinkles, he was still very fit and nimble for his age, with just a slight forward hunch in his neck, which caused his long grey hair to fall over his face. He tended to only trim his hair and his beard once or twice a year, which gave him the messy, careworn look of an elderly human, but his bright blue eyes never missed a thing.

Invisible Watcher Grambold

Chapter Eleven
Singing Fairies

The green dragon set off in the direction that Oak-ley had indicated, he walked for a further six days before the five-peaked mountain became visible. The night before their arrival at the mountain, No-Name, Sunny and Blue talked about how excited they were at the prospect of meeting the fairies.

Grambold, as usual, was hiding nearby and he could hear their conversation quite clearly. Having never heard of fairies before, he decided to stay well out of the way again, just in case the fairies could sense his presence. When the green dragon reached the base of the five peaks, he spent a lot of time searching, but could not find any sign of the fairies. Disappointed, the green dragon decided to lay down and rest for a little while.

Almost as soon as they'd lain down, Blue started whingeing. "I'm really sad that we can't find the fairies! Oak-ley said they loved to play and sing. What a shame we cannot find them!"

The fairies had remained in hiding, but when they heard the dragon speak of Oak-ley, several came out from their hiding places and flew around the dragon's three heads. Their wings looked just like butterflies, each pair made up of wonderful colours. All the fairies appeared to be very small girls, with smiley faces and tiny pointed ears.

The fairies wore shiny clothing made of fine material and patterns of silvery leaves fitted closely to their upper bodies. Their short, flowing skirts were made of the same material.

No-Name spoke first, and kept his voice soft and gentle. "Hello, tiny ones."

One of the fairies landed on top of his head and spoke in a child-like, high-pitched voice. "Hello! We were afraid when you arrived at first, until you mentioned Oak-ley. You must be friendly, if you know her."

"Yes, we are friendly and we saw Oak-ley only six days ago, she told us where you lived. We are on a quest, searching for a name for me. What is your name?" asked No-Name.

The fairy on top of No-Name's head looked a little worried when she replied. "My name is Red Tip. I'm sorry, but I do not think we can help you find a name, it took us a great deal of time trying to find names for ourselves."

No-Name shook his head quickly, keen to reassure the little fairy. "Do not worry about that; we came to find you because Oak-ley told us so much about you, not because we thought you could help with my name. Where do you live?"

Red Tip

Red Tip answered. "Our grotto is in the hollow of an oak tree; it grew from one of Oak-ley's acorns. Lots of very large toadstools grow in the hollow of the tree and we live inside them. They make perfect homes for us and fireflies provide us with all the light we need."

Blue was much happier now he'd seen the fairies, and quickly introduced himself. "Hi, I'm Blue! We are so glad to meet you."

One little fairy who was hovering close to Blue replied in almost a whisper. "That's almost the same as my name! I'm Blue Tip."

Sunny smiled broadly. "My name is Sunny."

Another fairy who was hovering near Sunny spoke up. "I'm Yellow Tip."

"It's a pleasure to meet you, Yellow Tip. Oak-ley told us that you all have beautiful voices – would you sing for us?"

Another pretty fairy spoke up. "My name is Green Tip. I'll gather some more fairies together, so we can sing for you." With that, she shouted in a high-pitched squeal and more fairies came out of hiding, forming a group. They began to sing and No-Name, Sunny and Blue began to move in time with their singing.

When the fairies stopped, the green dragon clapped his hands together and No-Name smiled. "That was so wonderful, thank you!

Your song sounded sweeter than the birds."

The fairies giggled loudly, their little hands covered their mouths and their shoulders rose and fell with utter glee.

All the other fairies came out of hiding and began to dance and sing; and soon, everyone was having so much fun. Some of the fairies played tag, some played hide and seek, and the dragon joined in all the games. There was more chattering and giggling than the green dragon had ever heard before.

Grambold remained hidden in the shadows, being careful not to be seen, but there was a broad smile on his face, because the green dragon and the fairies were having so much fun.

Chapter Twelve
A Special New Friend

The dragon and the fairies played together for a very long time, and the dragon had just sat down to rest when Red Tip came close to No-Name and whispered in his ear. "You've proven yourself to be a real friend of ours – would you like to meet a Unicorn Pegasus?"

"What is a Unicorn Pegasus?" No-Name asked.

"We call it a Unicorn for short. It's a special white horse, which has wings and he can fly."

No-Name was very interested, but he couldn't imagine a horse with wings. "What are the wings made from?"

Red-Tip looked around the woods, as though searching for the right answer. "The wings look very much like bird's wings."

Sunny and Blue responded together. "You mean they're made of feathers?"

"Yes, that's right," Red Tip answered, and nodded vigorously. "He also has one horn that grows from the centre of his head and the horn possesses great magical powers. Unicorns do not talk, but we can hear his thoughts and he understands what everyone says, even though he can't speak."

Sunny and Blue spoke excitedly. "He sounds magical with his horn and wings! When can we meet him?"

Red Tip looked at several of her friends before she spoke shyly. "Stay here tonight, because he is due to come and visit us in the morning. You'll need to be ready just before the sun comes up."

"Okay, we will be ready," No-Name agreed.

Even though the green dragon was very tired, he didn't sleep very well because he was so excited about meeting the Unicorn.

The following morning, while it was still dark, the green dragon was woken by Yellow Tip. She indicated they should follow her and stopped under a large tree beside a clearing. "Please stay in the shadows until I go and talk with the Unicorn about you. Only come out if I call you, please. If he does not wish to meet you, do not come out."

"Okay we will do as you ask, but please say nice things about us because we want to meet him so much," Sunny and Blue agreed with a big yawn.

Yellow Tip nodded. "Of course I will."

Grambold was awake, but he didn't dare move from his hiding place. Instead, he just lay there and watched the scene unfold before him.

Only a few of the fairies, including Red Tip,

Yellow Tip, Blue Tip and Green Tip waited with the green dragon. Suddenly there was a rush of air as the Unicorn came down to land, his wings flapped very swiftly. He landed and carried on running for a short distance before he slowed down to a walking speed. It seemed apparent to the green dragon that Unicorns needed plenty of space to land and take off.

No-Name, Sunny and Blue studied the curious creature. The unicorn's body was white and his large, feathered wings were even whiter, which grew out of the Unicorn's back they were covered in thousands of soft down feathers. His mane and tail were whiter than white; in fact, they looked more like silver. The single horn that grew from the centre of his head sparkled magically and it seemed to be made of glass and gold, shining in the first glimmer of sunrise.

Red Tip flew across to the Unicorn and chattered with him for a short time. Red-Tip glanced around at the green dragon, but to his disappointment, did not call for them to approach. As promised, the dragon waited in the shadows, and Red Tip flew back to join him.

"I'm sorry but the Unicorn does not want to meet you, he says he's too afraid of you because you are a dragon with three heads."

Pegasus Unicorn

No-Name responded solemnly, ensuring he spoke loudly enough for the Unicorn to hear. "We have lived our lives simply on a farm, and we were brought up by a man named Miller. We've only just learnt that we are a dragon, you have nothing to fear from us, even with our three heads."

Red Tip flew back over to the Unicorn and seemed to listen carefully, although the green dragon could hear no sound.

"He has changed his mind and he will meet you, but all the fairies must come along as well." With that she made a high-pitched noise and all the fairies came flying out and gathered around the Unicorn.

The green dragon walked slowly towards the group and stopped a short distance away from them. No-Name spoke in a gentle, quiet voice. "Thank you for letting us meet you. I have no name, but this is Sunny and this is Blue."

The Unicorn studied them for a moment or two, before he inclined his head, very regally.

No-Name continued. "We are thirty years old, but please, look upon us as if we were newly born as we have only just discovered what we are. We started on a quest several weeks ago, to find me a name, and when we met Oak-ley, she was the one who told us that we are a dragon. We have already met several mystical creatures.

That's why we wanted to meet you."

Green Tip was close to the Unicorn and seemed to be listening carefully to his thoughts. It seemed that he could relay his thoughts, in much the same way as Blue and Sunny could share their thoughts. After a minute or two, she flew to No-Name and relayed the Unicorn's message. "Unicorns do not have names, but he is aware of your desire to find one. He was moved by your kind words, and he is glad he decided to meet you."

"Thank you," No-Name said.

"He wants you to know that we fairies are not of the same age as any of you, we are always young and stay child-like throughout our entire lives. To communicate through us is very difficult."

Sunny and Blue replied. "Perhaps you could answer our questions by nodding or shaking your head?"

The Unicorn nodded his head up and down, just once.

Sunny and Blue spoke together. "Does your horn fall off and re-grow, the same way as a deer's?"

The Unicorn shook his head from side to side.

Sunny and Blue then asked another question. "Can you fly a for a long time?"

Again, the Unicorn shook his head from

side to side.

"Do you eat grass, hay and oats?" No-Name asked.

The Unicorn nodded. Green Tip hovered near him and she listened to the Unicorn for a moment or two. "He also eats leaves from a special tree," she explained.

Sunny and Blue were thinking back and forth to one another about the power of the horn. They both asked together. "What power does your horn possess?"

Blue Tip called out "It has the power to heal and to make bad things good."

"We hope you are not alone," No-Name asked quietly. "Are there others of your kind in the forest?"

The Unicorn nodded.

Blue Tip said "He has a mate."

"Have you anything you want to ask us?" Sunny and Blue asked.

Blue Tip listened carefully to the Unicorn before she spoke. "He says not for now, but maybe next time you could meet his mate. He must be on his way, before the sun gets any higher in the sky."

The dragon walked very slowly and cautiously towards the Unicorn and reached out, gently stroking his neck and back. No-Name whispered in the Unicorn's ear. "It's been a real pleasure to meet you, and we look forward to seeing you both next time."

The Unicorn didn't pull away immediately; instead, he stood there, he seemed to enjoy the affectionate gesture. The dragon slowly moved away and the Unicorn began to run and soon took off flying into the distance, his huge wings flapped in the breeze.

"That was quite an experience," Sunny and Blue said, both turned to the fairies. "Thank you so much for introducing us to him. We are sorry, but we must also be on our way."

All the fairies said goodbye and waved frantically as the three-headed dragon walked away. He stopped and turned to wave one last time before he disappeared into the woods. "We will come back to see you again!" Sunny and Blue called.

***

Grambold had thought to himself. The three-headed dragon had met more mystical creatures in these past few weeks than he had in three hundred years. Was this the reason he was drawn to them? Grambold was feeling more and more as if he knew the three-headed dragon very well indeed, and wished he could talk to them, but he had to keep the promise he had made to himself not to get involved with others.

Chapter Thirteen
The Red Dragon

There was no need to make any decisions regarding which way to go next, because in the distance, they could see a very high, ghostly mountain with a single, pointed white peak. It was so high, it seemed to disappear into the clouds, so they walked towards it.

After they had walked for two days straight, Sunny and Blue spoke. "That's one big mountain, it seems to be getting higher and higher, but we don't seem to be getting any closer."

Grambold knew exactly where they were going and he had a good idea who would be there, but he decided he would stay well behind and watch from a distance. He must soon find a cave and write up all he had seen over the last few weeks; he was getting farther and farther behind with his work.

When the green dragon walked, he tended not to talk, saving all his breath and energy for walking swiftly, only stopping to sleep at night. During the day, he rested for a short while at midday and ate small morsels of food, which he'd found along the way. Sometimes, he found some berries, or some fruit or even edible roots and the dragon relied on drinking water from streams to keep from getting thirsty.

The dragon had walked for four more days, but he'd hardly noticed that his walking seemed quicker and quieter, and the farting and belching which accompanied his steady stride had almost stopped, too. It was another sunny day and in the distance, his eyes were drawn to a small red spot coming closer and closer towards them, flying through the brilliant blue sky.

They stood in silence as the small red dot gradually grew to reveal a red dragon.

"This must be the red dragon Oak-ley told us about," No-name suggested.

The red dragon flew down majestically and landed just to the side of them. Her wings folded away, and she suddenly blew out a large plume of fire and smoke which left the air smelling of brimstone. The heat was intense, and as the smoke cleared, the red dragon spoke. "Well, what have we here? You look rather worried for a green dragon with… yes, if my eyes do not deceive me… three heads! Where have you come from? Who the devil are you? And what are you doing here?"

All this was said in one large breath of the now-cold air, before the red dragon continued, sounding rather stern. "I thought I was the only living dragon on this planet – are one of you going to say something, or can't any of you speak?"

"Yes!" No-Name responded, thinking how stunning the red dragon looked. She had the same red eyes as he did. "We can speak, but you didn't give us much chance to reply. You seemed a bit excited. This is Sunny and this is Blue. I have no name, and we have been on a quest to find one. We aren't as surprised to see you as you are to see us. We have come a long way, from the three-peaked mountain. What is your name?"

"You are right; I am surprised to see you – something not just mythical but also magical. My name is Re-ad and I am so glad to meet you."

"Sorry, but we are not magical in any way," No-Name responded. "Have you lived here long?"

"Yes, ever since I hatched over thirty years ago," Re-ad answered.

"That makes us about the same age," Sunny and Blue said.

"Would you like to fly back with me to my den, where we can talk?" Re-ad asked.

"We cannot fly," Sunny, Blue and No-Name replied together.

"I can see you have wings – why can't you fly?" asked Re-ad.

"We never imagined we could and only found a short time ago, from Oak-ley, that we're a dragon," No-Name replied.

"I have never heard of Oak-ley, but I assume she is a tree. So, you cannot breathe fire, either?" Re-ad asked.

"No, we cannot breathe fire! And yes, Oak-ley is a very old and wise oak tree," Sunny and Blue announced.

"Why don't you walk with us for a while, we have lots to talk about," No-Name suggested.

"I'm sure we do, but do you know what is strange? I have spent most of my life searching for other dragons, and you just come walking into my valley."

"That's fate," Sunny and Blue replied knowingly. Miller had told them all about fate.

Re-ad looked puzzled. "My den is at the base of that snow-covered peak, a short way up the valley. I'll show you the way, and we can chat as we go along."

Chapter Fourteen
Re-ad's Amazing Den

Everyone began to talk at once – it seemed four dragon heads had lots of things to talk about.

"Why don't we take turns to ask questions," No-Name suggested.

"That sounds like a good idea," said Re-ad. "Can I go first? There are three of you and only one of me."

"That seems fair," Sunny and Blue replied.

"Is it nice where you live?" Re-ad asked.

Sunny and Blue sighed. "It's very flat with only a few trees and not half as nice as your beautiful green valley."

As they continued walking No-Name asked, "What is snow?"

Re-ad pointed to the white-topped peak. "That white covering on top of the mountain. It's very cold up there and when it rains down here, it falls as snow on the peak."

"We must get to see that," said Sunny and Blue.

The three heads were so busy looking at the beauty all around them, they found it hard to talk at the same time. The valley was green and lush, with trees and wild flowers growing everywhere. A small river ran through the valley and sparkled like silver. It was so different from the area around the farm. All three heads appreciated the beautiful scenery and it made them feel good inside.

Re-ad pointed to the far end of the valley. "That's where my den is. You can't see it yet, but we'll be there shortly."

They were soon standing outside a large, almost perfectly round hole which looked as if it had been cut out of the rock face by a giant, mechanical diamond-cutting machine.

Re-ad invited them in. "Come in, it's bigger inside than it looks," she announced. They followed her in to discover the walls were covered with crystals, diamonds and large sheets of polished silver. Gold streaks which resembled large tree roots filled in between the gaps, as if some mystical artist had painted it.

"We have never seen anything like this!" Sunny and Blue exclaimed. As they continued walking further in, the entrance expanded into a massive cave. The walls and high roof were even more beautiful than the entrance.

It was very light inside and Re-ad informed them of the reason why. "The light in here is reflected into the cave by all the crystals and diamonds from outside. Some of the crystals give off a soft green light when the sun goes down at night, so it never gets really dark in here."

The three-headed dragon looked around the cave in wonder, marvelling at its beauty. Best of all, the cave was not too hot or too cold, but just the right temperature for dragons.

Chapter Fifteen

Re-ad's Freezer

Re-ad settled down in a cosy corner gesturing to the three-headed dragon to come closer. "Please come and join me so we can talk; make yourselves comfortable."

The green dragon did as he was told and soon felt quite at home.

Re-ad asked the first question. "Where do you come from?"

Sunny and Blue answered. "We live in a large barn next to an old mill, near a mountain with three peaks."

"Who looked after you after you hatched?" No-Name asked.

"My mother; she was black, tall and very lean – in fact, she was named Ever-lean," Re-ad answered.

"How wonderful that must have been for you," Sunny and Blue said together.

"It was," Re-ad agreed. "Who brought you up after you'd hatched?"

Blue answered. "A farmer named Miller, but he died about twenty years after he found us. We carried on doing the same things he did, working on his farm. It was all we knew."

Sunny had a question of his own. "When do

you eat? Our tummy is rumbling, we have not eaten much for weeks."

"You must think me a poor host," Re-ad exclaimed. "I'll get something from my freezer."

"Freezer? What's that?" Sunny and Blue asked in unison.

"Come along; I'll show you." Re-ad gestured to the three-headed dragon and he followed Re-ad along a narrow, low, dark tunnel. It sloped up steeply and it took a while to get to a small, poorly lit and very cold cave. Ice could be seen on the walls and roof and the green dragon shuddered.

"This is my freezer, I use it to keep my meat fresh for weeks," Re-ad explained. She gathered up some meat that was frozen solid, and put it onto a large golden plate. The cave was too small to allow Re-ad to pass by the green dragon, so she told No-Name, Sunny and Blue to return to the cave and she would follow behind.

"I'll defrost the meat on the way," Re-ad explained. The dark tunnel lit up as Re-ad breathed out a burst of fire to defrost the frozen lump of meat.

They sat back down in the corner of the cave and the green dragon didn't want to admit he'd never eaten raw meat before. He waited and watched Re-ad as she picked up a slither of the meat in her talons, tossed her head back and popped it into her mouth. She didn't chew the meat, instead letting it slip straight down her throat in one whole piece. The green dragon copied what Re-ad had done, and let the piece of meat slither down his throat.

"How do you like the meat?" Re-ad questioned.

"It's very nice the way you eat it," Sunny and Blue announced together. All three heads laughed, and soon the meat was all gone.

"It's only fair that you ask the next question, Re-ad," said Blue. "After all, you've provided us with a lovely meal." For a short time, they questioned each other and discovered a lot about their very different lives.

"How is it that you can fly and breathe fire?" No-Name asked.

"Is that two questions?" asked Re-ad, with a bright smile. When she saw the green dragon start to blush and stutter, she shook her head and laughed. "That's okay, I'm happy to answer two questions. As you have seen, I eat raw meat, and I drink some of the black oil which seeps up from the ground and inhale a small amount of gas that also comes from underground. I keep some sparklight between my teeth – one piece in the top set and one piece in the bottom set." She opened her mouth and showed them, pointing with one of her claws. "When I snap my mouth shut, the sparklight strike each other and create a large spark, which ignites the mixture of gas and oil that I fetch up out of my tummy. It only ignites when it reaches the pocket of air just inside my mouth."

"That is so clever! We would never have thought of that," said Blue and Sunny.

"You're so amazing!" the three heads all agreed.

Re-ad looked quite embarrassed. "No, no – that's just what I do because I'm a dragon." She hurriedly changed the subject. "My mother taught me how to fly and I look forward to teaching you, but you need to be aware of the dangers of flying."

"What dangers are you referring to?" No-Name demanded.

"Volcanoes," Re-ad announced ominously.

"What are volcanoes?" Blue asked.

"It's a mountain which spews out red hot, flowing rock. It can start off with a big explosion which shoots up high into the sky, and it fills an area with smoke and flames."

"That sounds dangerous," No-Name muttered. "But I would still like to see one."

"Once you learn how to fly, you will get to see one, but only from a safe distance," Re-ad warned. "It is very dangerous; an explosion can happen at any moment and very suddenly. My mother was killed by one, that's why I stay well away from volcanoes." Re-ad gazed down at her feet, she was obviously feeling sad, thinking about the loss of her mother.

"We are sorry for your loss and it is right that you remember your mother with sadness and fond memories. We still remember Miller, he was like a father to us," No-Name said in a quiet voice. He decided a change of subject was in order. "Have you ever heard the fairies sing?"

Re-ad lifted her head. "Fairies! I have never seen or met any fairies, what are they?"

The three heads took it in turns to tell Re-ad about their meeting with the fairies and she listened intently. Soon her sorrow had diminished and the cave was full of laughter again, as both dragons chuckled at the tales of the fairies' antics.

Chapter Sixteen

The First Night in Re-ad's Cave

The cave was very comfortable and Sunny and Blue eventually fell fast asleep. Re-ad and No-Name whispered to one another for a short while longer.

"What things do you enjoy doing?" Re-ad asked.

"Not much really, it's hard work farming, but very rewarding when you see the crops growing. We enjoy preparing and cooking the food we eat; making the bread requires co-ordination, because the ingredients must be measured out precisely and mixed together carefully – even though we try, it's still a messy job, flour tends to go everywhere and the dough can get sticky and gooey. It's still hard to believe the finished product can look and taste so good. We have always worked well together." No-Name watched Re-ad for a moment before he whispered again. "What about you?   What do you enjoy?"

Re-ad smiled. "I only come in the cave to sleep, I really love flying – the feeling of freedom and the world below looks so beautiful. I love being outside. I have spent lots of time searching for other dragons. I've just realised how lonely I've been, since my mother died five years ago. You are so lucky having each other."

"We think so, too," No-Name said.

"I think the major difference in our lives is that you are used to working on the farm. I don't work at all and in the time that you've been travelling, you have met and made many friends. I have none."

"Miller instilled in us the need to work hard – only then can you really enjoy the rewards and yes, we have met many mystical creatures during our travels. The Unicorn was quite special."

"What was he like?" Re-ad asked.

"He's very much like a white horse, but one who has large feathered wings that help him fly. A single magical horn grows from the centre of his head, and he and his mate spend a lot of time in hiding," Re-ad exclaimed.

"No wonder I have never seen him."

"It's not just him you've missed while flying around – walking does have some benefits." No-Name commented.

Re-ad put a flat claw to her mouth and yawned loudly. "It's time to sleep, I am so tired, my brain has been in overdrive."

"So has ours – and we have three." No-Name grinned. "Good night, Re-ad."

"Good night," she said and then smiled

warmly. "That sounds so good, having someone to say good night to."

"Things will be so different now, Re-ad," No-Name answered softly. "You are no longer alone – you have a friend in us."

Chapter Seventeen
Preparing to Fly

They woke up together and with the cave full of light, Re-ad led the way outside. With just a few extra steps forwards, her wings came out and flapped a few times and she was quickly climbing up into the sky.

She swooped and circled around gracefully, then she flew so high they could hardly see her, getting smaller and smaller until she was just a speck in the distance. Suddenly she shot down, faster and faster like a speeding arrow, until she almost came to a stop and landed gently beside them.

"That was so wonderful to watch," Sunny and Blue said. "We wished that we could have joined you up there, but we are not as sleek and slim as you and we don't know how to fly."

"What are you talking about? That's not what I see," said Re-ad. "You have a perfect, slender body which fits with the fact that you have three heads."

The three heads looked down and could hardly believe what they saw; their once-fat body was slim, the lumpy bumpy tail was sleek and smooth, even the spikes had worn away until it looked like a very large snake's tail. All the scales along their sides and back were perfectly shaped, each one lying flat and smooth where they followed the contours of their slim body beneath.

"By golly gosh bump, we are slim!" all three shouted with glee and danced a little jig.

"Now do you believe you could fly?" asked Re-ad.

"We do!" they replied together.

"Now you need to prepare; drink the oil and top up with the gas and fit the sparklight into your teeth – then you can start to learn how to fly."

"That's not quite how we do things," said Sunny and Blue.

"No, it's not," No-Name agreed.

"We must all agree that this is what we want," Sunny and Blue continued.

They all shouted together loudly. "We do! We do want to fly!"

"Well, that was a quick decision," said Re-ad, smiling broadly. "Follow me," she ordered, and led the green dragon to some dried shrubs. She removed the shrubs to reveal a large, black smelly pool of oil. "Drink this, until you feel just a quarter full – no more," Re-ad ordered.

Each head took small sips and when their tummy felt as if it were a quarter full, Sunny and Blue both spoke. "That's it, we have had enough."

"Good, now come this way," Re-ad said, as she led them along the valley until they reached a small hollow in the ground. "Now," she told them. "Go down into the hollow and stick your head into any holes you find, breathe in very deeply through your nostrils and mouth. You will smell and taste the gas on the back of your tongue. Be careful not to take in too much, and only one of you should do this because you only need a small amount, so it just covers the oil."

"Shall I do this part?" No-Name asked.

"Yes!" Sunny and Blue agreed. The green dragon walked into the hollow and it didn't take long before he returned.

"You must have picked a good supply of gas, to have topped up so quickly," said Re-ad.

"I took a few sniffs at different holes, and chose the strongest smelling one," No-Name explained.

"Here is some sparklight you can use," said Re-ad, pointing to a crack in the side of the mountain. Each head put some between their teeth and looked at Re-ad expectantly.

"And now, you're ready to learn how to fly," she announced.

***

In the distance, hidden in a cave and with the invisibility cloak carefully tucked around him to ensure he'd be completely invisible, Grambold watched intently. He could hardly wait to see the green dragon's first attempt at flying.

Chapter Eighteen
The Flying Lesson

The flying lesson began at midday, because it was the hottest part of the day, Re-ad explained.

"Any hot air rising will help you fly, you can't just flap your wings and expect to fly off – you need to practice flapping while you're still standing on the ground, so you can get used to how your wings feel. This will help you judge how much you'll need to flap to take off. Try and hover, with your toes just touching the ground and that will help you gain your balance. When you feel ready, flap your wings harder and keep flapping until you're flying upwards. Use your tail to steer, and your wings can also be waved stiffly up or down to help adjust your direction. Tilt the front of your wings down towards the ground and that movement will direct you downwards. Tilt them up and you'll go up; keep your body and tail flat out behind you. If you try to fly with your legs and body leaning downwards, it will be very hard to fly, you only do this when you want to come down to land. Now, is there anything you want to ask me?"

"That's a lot to remember," Sunny said

nervously.

"Once you're at a good height, you can stop flapping your wings and spread them out as far as they can go and you'll be able to glide around in circles. I'll be close by, to talk you through any problems you might have."

Blue piped up. "We have one problem. It sounds as if we must make lots of decisions quickly. Sunny and I are linked by more than just our body – we think what each other thinks and most of the time, we say the same things, but No-Name doesn't share this link with us. He's always been able to think faster than us, but not the same way as us."

Re-ad was surprised. "Why do you see this as a problem? You have always lived like this – you communicate to one another all the time and that is all you need to do when flying. Believe it or not, flying is as easy as walking – once you know how, it all becomes second nature. Walking on two legs is harder than you think; it must have taken you a while to learn and I bet you can't even remember doing it. Why not break down the elements of flying, so you each do what you're best at, then put it all together as you do when you make a loaf of bread?"

"That sounds good!" Sunny and Blue agreed.

"Let's do this!" No-Name, Blue and Sunny

all shouted together. They were now quite determined to learn how to fly, and master another new skill!

"Are you all set?" asked Re-ad.

Sunny opened his mouth and out came a large flame.

"Awesome!" Blue and No-Name breathed.

"No more fire breathing!" Re-ad shouted. She made them stand on a small hill and then bellowed instructions. "Well! What are you waiting for! Face into the wind because it will help you take off."

The green dragon's bat-like wings unfurled and started to flap. They were a bit floppy because they had been folded up for so many years, so it took a while for them to unfurl and fill up with power and blood. Then the air seemed to be picking the green dragon off the ground. He stayed there for some time, hovering like a hummingbird, and then lifted off totally and climbed up into the brilliant blue sky.

Re-ad flew close by, giving hints on anything she thought would be useful. She need not have worried, because the green dragon was in complete control and was swooping, diving and gliding as if he had been doing it all his life.

"Now we know the true wonders of flying,

words can't explain these feelings," said Sunny and Blue.

"I will be sad to land," Blue said.

After a good while longer, Re-ad spoke again. "It will be getting dark soon. We must land now, because we might need to replenish the oil. Your back and shoulder muscles are not used to all this exercise and that can cause lots of pain. It's best not to do too much on your first flight."

When the two dragons came down to land, No-Name spoke. "We have still got plenty of oil and gas. Couldn't we fly for a little while longer?"

Re-ad shook her head firmly. "We must eat a little now and you need to rest. Tomorrow we will try flying out to the sea."

In the cave that night, it was a long time before the shadows of sleep came over the green dragon. The three heads could not stop talking about the experience of flying, the exhilaration and the feeling of freedom they'd experienced, and the beauty of the landscape below them as they flew and soared in the cloudless blue sky.

"Thank you for changing our lives so dramatically, Re-ad," No-Name said.

"I have done very little," she replied. "Sunny and Blue deserve the credit for bringing you on this quest; they unwittingly brought you to find part of your destiny."

***

In his hiding place with the cloak now removed, Grambold thought for a long time, recalling the way the dragons had flown so beautifully for several hours. He had been delighted by the sight of the two dragons flying with such grace and beauty. *Something else to write about,* he thought to himself.

Chapter Nineteen

Discovering the Sea

The green dragon and Re-ad spent hours talking together, like small, excited children, and their voices echoed through every corner of the cave. Eventually, the cave fell silent and the two dragons fell into a very peaceful sleep. The three heads seemed to nod back and forth as if they were still in flight, but all were resting on the floor, fast asleep and with happy smiles on their faces.

The cave had been in bright light for several hours before Re-ad opened her eyes, and when she did, she quickly woke the green dragon and hurried him out of the cave. "Well!" she said. "You need to do something about all the farting that you did in the night, you must learn some control."

"We have never bothered before," said No-Name. "We couldn't stop it from happening."

"I should have told you that at the end of the day; it's always best to release most of the gas before you go to sleep; that way you can control the farting better."

"Now you tell us!" Sunny and Blue said, both rolling their eyes.

"We felt really bad about it, especially in your company, we had noticed that you did not trump at all."

Re-ad didn't tell them that she often trumped when she was flying – no lady dragon would admit to that. "Let's eat some meat and get stocked up on oil and gas, ready for our long flight today. We'll fly across the land to the sea we'll go the shortest way; but you can go in any direction and you'll eventually reach the sea – it completely surrounds Pangreat."

"What do you mean, about the sea being around Pangreat?" No-Name asked.

"My mother told me that the planet was round and the land was surrounded by the sea. The best way to see it, is to fly up as high as possible. We could do that another day," Re-ad explained.

"Do we need the gas and oil to fly?" No-Name asked.

"I have always thought so, but now that you mention it, I'm not so sure," answered Re-ad. "My mother never told me and it never occurred to me to ask; other than defrosting the meat, I have never used the flame for anything else."

"I must say that the smoke and fire looked impressive, but it didn't seem to do anything useful," No-Name said jokingly.

"When we get back from our flight, shall we investigate?" Re-ad asked.

"Sounds good to us," Sunny and Blue replied.

It didn't take long before they were ready for the long flight, and Re-ad led the way up into the cloudless sky. They flew for several hours, and covered a much greater distance than the green dragon had managed when he was walking.

***

Far below, Grambold watched them disappear into the distance. He decided he should get back to the cave and spend the day catching up on his writing, because he suspected the two dragons wouldn't be back until just before dark.

***

After some time flying, Re-ad suddenly shouted. "Look! That's the sea!"

They could see the colours of the land ahead the green suddenly turned gold, and then a line of blue appeared where the land met the sea. A faint line could also be seen in the far distance, where the sea met the sky.

Re-ad brought them down to land on a

sandy beach. "We will fly out across the sea for a short way and then turn around and come back here. Remember, we need to keep the land in sight."

The two dragons took off and flew out for miles over the calm blue sea. A short time later, a large island could be seen in the direction they were flying.

"Let's land on that island," Re-ad suggested. "It's a bit strange though – I don't remember seeing it the last time I came this way."

Chapter Twenty
The Mysterious Island

When the dragons landed, the whole island seemed to move a little beneath their feet. Suddenly, it rose up out of the sea and got bigger and bigger with each passing second. Both dragons were shocked to discover that rather than an island, they had in fact, landed on a very large sea turtle.

The turtle was surprised to discover the two dragons riding on its back. "Hello," the turtle said in a soft, sweet voice. "Are you okay?"

"Yes, we are okay," Re-ad said. "I'm sorry if we startled you; we thought you were an island. I'm Re-ad, what's your name?"

"My name is Myrtle. I am over seven hundred years old and I have seen you flying over the sea before. You look so majestic when you fly, not unlike the fish who live and swim under the sea."

Sunny and Blue introduced themselves and told her they lived near the three-peaked mountain not far from the sea. "Our other head doesn't have a name, so we have always called him No-Name."

"I have never seen the fish under the sea," Re-ad added.

"Would you like to see some?" Myrtle asked.

They all nodded enthusiastically. "We would love to," Sunny and Blue agreed.

"I'll be happy to show you. You can climb inside my shell and I will take you down to see them."

Myrtle peeled back a large piece of her skin, to reveal an opening into her shell. The two dragons climbed inside the shell and Myrtle covered the opening again with the layer of skin. "Move over to the right, where there is more room," she suggested.

Without another word, Myrtle dived to the bottom of sea. The dragons could see everything, through a small translucent section of her shell. They stared at the wonders of the deep, the light from the sun above made the sea look blue and clear.

Fish of many colours swam everywhere, and beautiful coral spread out like a rich, multi-coloured carpet beneath them. They saw sharks, tiger fish, starfish, lobsters and crabs, and they marvelled at a great white whale as it swam lazily by. There was so much diverse life in the sea it was mind-blowing, and many of the fish seemed to swim around majestically. Some swam around individually or in small groups, others swam in massive shoals; moving together in unison, they would suddenly change direction without breaking up their group.

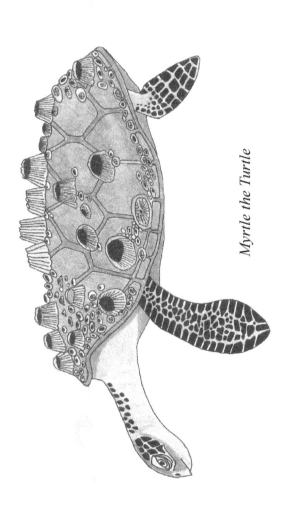

Myrtle the Turtle

Myrtle told them that the fish were meant to resemble one large fish, which is exactly what they looked like. What was amazing, was that they never collided into one another. Different species of fish swam together in the same way, as if they were joined together by invisible threads. A small pod of dolphins swam by and they breached out of the water. They seemed to be talking to each other, with lots of clicks and squeaks.

Myrtle went further out along the sea bed, before she dropped suddenly, diving down along what appeared to be a deep cliff. Out of the grey, murky depths came several giant fish of different shapes and sizes, any single one of them big enough to swallow Myrtle in one easy gulp.

Blue called out. "Are we in danger of becoming a fish supper?"

Myrtle giggled. "No need to worry, they all eat krill and plankton."

"You could have told us that sooner," Blue said, sounding very relieved.

The air in the shell started to get thin and the two dragons found it harder and harder to breathe. Myrtle realised what was happening and quickly surfaced and let them out. They were relieved to climb back onto her shell and gulped in great lungs full of the fresh air. Both dragons were breathing normally again within a few minutes.

"Are you all right?" Myrtle asked, sounding concerned. "Just breathe in and out deeply and you will be fine. We were down a little too long, so the air in my shell got bad. I hope you don't mind, but I've brought you close to the three-peaked mountain where you live."

No-Name wanted to know how it was possible to have come so far so quickly and Myrtle explained that the sea was shaped like her flipper, separating the land on both sides.

Re-ad was surprised too, and told them that she never flew further than she could manage to return in the same day. Now she was much farther away from home, and she sounded a little worried by this fact.

Chapter Twenty-One
At Last, a Name Is Found

No-Name reassured Re-ad that she didn't need to worry because she was in safe hands with them. He turned to speak to Myrtle. "That was such a wonderful experience! Could we do it again, next time we meet?" he asked.

"It would be a pleasure to take you down again, you both seemed to appreciate the wonders of the sea so much. I must tell you something, No-Name. When I first saw you, I couldn't help but notice your head with the three peaks, and I believe they look like a crown."

Sunny and Blue called out. "We can see the three-peaked mountain! Let's get going!" The green dragon took off, wings flapping, and No-Name called out to Re-ad. "It's okay, Re-ad – follow us!"

"See you again!" they all called back to Myrtle from the skies above the massive turtle.

Sunny and Blue spoke at once. "Well that was very enlightening, in more ways than one. Myrtle was right about the top of your head looking like a crown. Do you think that King should be your name?"

"Perhaps. Do you really think so?" No-Name asked.

"Yes, yes we do!" Sunny and Blue said excitedly.

"I thought so too, but I couldn't bring myself to say anything about it to you," said No-Name. "I was afraid of what you might say; I should have known better."

Re-ad looked at the green dragon and thought to herself how special he was.

"This has been one of the best days of our lives! We will never forget it and we think we have completed our quest!" Sunny and Blue said.

"I must agree, I have just made another friend, and seen some wondrous sights," Re-ad said.

"And I have a great name," King added. "Let's go back to our farm now and then in the morning, we can treat Re-ad to one of our breakfasts."

"Is it far?" Re-ad asked.

"No, it's just over there," Sunny and Blue answered.

"It might help if you start to keep your necks and heads really close together, that way you'll be more streamlined," Re-ad suggested.

The green dragon took the lead and twisting their necks around each other, their heads came together naturally. Re-ad followed and after a short while, they glided down over the sea towards the land and as the two dragons circled around the side of the mountain, King shouted over the sound of the wind.

"Re-ad, this is much easier and we are going faster!" Then the two dragons came down to land, just outside the large barn on the farm.

Chapter Twenty-Two

A Warm Welcome

All five children came running out of the farm house and shouted excitedly. "They are back! They are back!"

The green dragon and all the children started to play around, skipping, and chatting to one another.

"Hello, how are you all?" King asked. "Where are your parents? What a welcoming party! This is our friend, Re-ad."

Susan turned to Re-ad. "Hello, my name is Susan." She turned her head towards the green dragon. "Mummy and daddy are out in the fields."

Each child introduced themselves in turn to Re-ad, before Stage and Act came running up to greet them. "We saw you fly in and hardly recognised who it was. You look so slim, and the way you were flying was wondrous to see! Who is your new friend?"

King looked over to where Re-ad stood, surrounded by all the children. "This is Re-ad, she taught us how to fly. Re-ad, this is Stage and Act."

"Well, I never expected this! You didn't tell me about all your friends! This is a lovely surprise! I am so glad to meet you all," Re-ad replied.

King just laughed out loud, saying, "There was so much going on, we just never got around to it. We talked Stage and his wife into staying here to look after the farm, so we could go on our quest to find me a name."

"It didn't take much to persuade us to stay, and it's turned out to be one of the best things we have ever done, we all love being here," Stage said, sounding a little wistful.

With that, King turned to look at each member of the family. "Would you and your family like to stay on here with us permanently? You can live in the farm house and we can all work together. I'm sure Sunny and Blue will want exactly the same thing."

"He knows us so well!" Sunny and Blue announced in unison. "Will you stay? It would make us so happy."

The whole family came together in a huddle, talking excitedly. It took only a few minutes before everyone turned around and Stage spoke happily. "We would love to stay here as one big happy family, and I should remind you – we still owe you a show."

King looked again at the family. "We have had a wondrous adventure and completed the quest. And I now have a name!"

Before he could say his name, Blue and

Sunny shouted together. "It's King! We would love to tell you more, but we are so very tired; we need to get off to the barn and get some sleep. We are shattered after flying so far."

"Yes, you will be tired, but once your muscles develop and you get used to flying, you won't be so badly affected." Re-ad explained. There was a twinkle in her eye when she spoke again. "You also need to go to sleep, and not spend half the night talking."

Everyone laughed and called good night to one another before a chorus of voices cried out together. "Good night, King!" They all burst out laughing and King smiled to himself, happy that at last, he had an identity of his own.

King spoke. "We need to get rid of all the gas and oil out of our tummies tonight, so tomorrow we can find out if we can fly without it."

Re-ad agreed and they found a large hole in the ground, where they poured the oil and then they let out all the gas, before both dragons walked into the barn.

"Have you anything to eat?" Re-ad asked. "I'm rather hungry."

Sunny and Blue answered. "Can you believe it; the pot is on the cooking range and we can smell the stew! The family must have kept it going for us all this time!"

"What wonderful people they are, but I think stew's a bit heavy for such a late supper," King responded. "We can have some eggs, milk and some corn on the cob – it will sustain us until morning."

Re-ad watched as the green dragon milked the cows. Sunny and Blue asked her if she would collect the eggs and the corn on the cob from the storehouse.

"Of course I will," Re-ad replied. A few minutes later, when they were eating and drinking, Re-ad smiled. "This is new food to me; the eggs slide down very well and the milk is so nice! The corn is sweet too. Altogether, it's a lovely snack."

The two dragons settled down for the night just a few minutes later and were soon fast asleep, and there was no belching or farting that night.

Chapter Twenty-Three
Re-ad's First Breakfast

In the morning, the green dragon and Re-ad got up very early. They took off and flew around for a little while and when they landed again, King spoke to Re-ad. "We had no problems flying without the oil and gas, but our shoulders are a little stiff."

"I had no problems either, and don't worry, the stiffness will wear off. It's because you're not used to flying."

"We feel much better without all that oil and gas sloshing around in our tummy," Blue and Sunny commented. "How about you?"

"To be honest, the flying seemed to be easier, but my tummy feels a bit strange and it was making growling noises as we flew," Re-ad responded thoughtfully.

Sunny laughed. "That's because it's empty! We need to get a good breakfast inside you."

King and Blue joined in the laughter. "Let's get cooking," they said together, and in no time at all, breakfast was ready.

Everyone was seated around the table and very happy. Re-ad was at one end of the long trestle table and the green dragon sat on its tail at the other end of the table. The youngest children sat closest to the dragons, with Stage and Act in the centre of the table, facing one another.

Susan leant forward and turned to the green dragon, speaking solemnly. "We have all missed you; even though we were only together for a short while, we felt that we had known you for ages."

"Whenever one of us went into the barn, we would gaze at bits of your egg shell – somehow it made us feel closer to you," Tame said shyly.

King, Sunny and especially Blue found these simple statements comforting, even though they evoked deep-felt emotions. Blue started to cry, and Sunny began crying too.

"Sorry, sorry, please forgive us. We are not sad, these are tears of joy – no one has ever said such nice things to us before. They were even more poignant, being spoken by children," King spluttered with tears in his eyes.

"Children are treasures and are a great part of our lives and our future," Act said softly. She turned to look at each head in turn and continued. "You are more kind and generous than anyone we have ever met and we all love you."

She got up and Stage joined her from the other side of the table. Both walked up to the green dragon and gave him a hug, before all five children jumped up and ran to join in.

Re-ad stayed at the end of the table, thinking again how wonderful the green dragon was and how lucky she was that he had come into her life.

"Hey, breakfast is getting cold! Let's eat it, because poor Re-ad is starving and so are we," King laughed.

Breakfast was eaten as idle chatter carried on between everyone.

"Do dragons breathe fire?" Tank asked Re-ad.

"We can, but we don't have to any more. Why do you ask?"

"Mummy told me that our farm was burnt down when fire fell from the sky, and I never knew where the fire came from."

Act interrupted. "Yes, I did say that, but I should have explained it a little better. The flames came from a volcano, Tank. Did you think it was a dragon?"

"No, I was just mixed up," Tank said.

"It must be difficult being parents, when there is so much to explain," King said softly to Act.

She shrugged. "We seem to be learning what to do as we go, not knowing if what we say or teach them is right or not."

King looked at Act and spoke knowingly.

"As a mother, I should think you have natural instincts to protect and love them, so whatever you decide to do for them, or say to them, is surely right – no one could ask for more. You decided to stay here for a better life for your children. We think that was a very good decision, and of course, there is the added bonus of two extra part-time parents, because we feel so much a part of your family."

Susan piped up. "We all feel that you're part of our family too, but I think it's time we put on our show for you."

"That's just what I was about to say," Stage said. "If we all work together, we can get all the farm work completed quickly."

"Yes! That's a great idea," Sunny and Blue responded. "We can celebrate being back home after completing our quest, and enjoy a few tankards of beer."

Chapter Twenty-Four
The Pantomime Play

The work was indeed carried out in double quick time, and just past midday, everyone was standing together outside the barn. Stage asked the two dragons to remain at the front of the farm house.

The family went inside the house and soon came out dressed in farm animal costumes. Tim, Tame and Tank were dressed to look like white swans or perhaps geese; it was hard to make out which. Tank looked a little uncomfortable in his tight outfit.

Susan was dressed as a horse, with an odd-looking, handmade horse's head. Mark was dressed to look like a chicken. Stage and Act, who looked like a farmer and his wife, turned to the two dragons and started to speak.

"Hello, we are Mr. and Mrs. Farmer and we have trouble with our little hen, she keeps hiding or gets lost. We need help to find her." Just then, Mark ran off and climbed into the wagon, pretending to be the missing chicken.

Stage went over to the horse and geese, asking them, "We have lost our only chicken again, can you help us find her?"

The three geese started to hiss and quack

and they waddled one behind each other, but they only went around and around in circles, not looking for the chicken anywhere.

Pretending to be the horse, Susan stomped and kicked the floor, snorting. Stage turned away from her and walked off. Susan then followed him wherever he went, not knowing what to do.

Sunny saw the funny side of it straight away, and started laughing. The scene before the two dragons got even more hilarious and confused. Act, on seeing the geese going around and around, and the horse just following Stage, waved her arms above her head and turning away from them all, walked off in the opposite direction, pretending to look for the hen in the wrong place.

Both Stage and Act started to call out. "Here little hen, here little hen – where are you?"

By this time, King and Blue were also laughing out loud. Re-ad wasn't sure what to do, but seeing the green dragon laughing so much, she started to titter and the sound soon built up into a big belly laugh.

The two dragons couldn't help themselves. Sunny stopped laughing and shouted, "She's over there!"

Stage and Act stopped moving and pretended they didn't see where Sunny had indicated, walking off in the wrong direction.

Both Sunny and Blue shouted out. "No! Over that way!"

Stage and Act still pretended they couldn't see where Sunny and Blue were pointing.

The two voices added more confusion and this time Stage and Act turned and walked towards one another, shouting for the hen.

Re-ad was still giggling, but managed to shout out. "No! She's over there!"

Stage and Act were still pretending to look for the hen, not at the dragons, so they acted as though they had no idea which way to go. Like the 'animals', they also seemed to be going around in circles.

By now, Blue and Sunny could hardly control their laugher.

King managed to muster a powerful voice. "Mr. and Mrs. Farmer, please stop!"

His voice was so loud, all the animals stopped instantly, as did Stage and Act. King spoke firmly again. "The hen is in the wagon."

Act and Stage went over to the wagon and started to look underneath it. This time, Re-ad managed to call out. "Silly farmers! The hen is in the wagon!"

Stage jumped up onto the wagon and Act began to clamber up onto it. Mark suddenly jumped down and ran off into the barn. Act called out. "I can't believe it, that's exactly where we wanted to put the hen in the first place!"

Stage started to clap, indicating this was the end of the play and the whole cast came and stood in a line in front of the dragons. They all bowed, and the two dragons clapped and shouted. "Hooray, hooray, hooray! Bravo!"

Four dragon heads can certainly make a lot of noise.

***

During supper that night, everyone was talking to one another, and the green dragon had three conversations going on at the same time. King was talking to Mark, and Sunny and Blue were talking to Tank and Tame.

Susan asked Re-ad if she thought her part in the play was the funniest.

"You were very funny following your father," Re-ad replied. In fact, I thought you were all hilarious! I have never laughed like that before."

"My costume was too small!" Tank muttered. "I thought you were all laughing at me!"

King stroked Tank's head and spoke to him tenderly. "Tank, you needn't have felt embarrassed. None of us noticed that your costume was too small. We were laughing at every one, you were all so very good."

"Thank you," Tank said and he smiled broadly and started to laugh, relieved by King's kind words.

"You were all very good," Sunny agreed. "We haven't had as much fun, since we were playing with the fairies."

Susan overheard, and asked, "What are fairies?"

Sunny and Blue explained the story of their meeting with the fairies.

"Were all the fairies the same age?" Susan asked.

"It was hard to tell, they certainly all looked about the same. Oak-ley told us they lived for two or three hundred years."

"Who is Oak-ley?" Tank asked.

King responded by telling everybody about Oak-ley.

"Did you meet any one else?" Tame asked curiously.

Sunny and Blue spoke together. "Myrtle the turtle, she was so big, at first we thought she was a very large island! We got inside her shell and she took us down to the bottom of the sea, it was a wondrous adventure and most memorable. But now we think it's time we had those beers and we have a special treat for everyone. Who wants to know what it is?"

"Me, me!" all the children shouted.

"Okay! We think it's a task for two," Sunny and Blue said. "Because Susan is the oldest and Tame is the youngest, they would suit the task very well. Go into the barn and enter the egg store, up on a high shelf you will see a dark brown jar, you need to bring it back to us."

A few minutes later, both children returned, Tame carrying the jar and she had a big smile on her face. She handed it to the green dragon, who opened it and placed it on the table. King asked them how they had gotten the jar down.

"I stood on Susan's shoulders and was able to get it down," Tame announced, sounding very proud.

"That was very clever and very brave of you, well done!" Act said with a bright smile.

"Please help yourselves to the biscuits," Sunny and Blue announced. "And we have one more task, which we think Tank should be able to do on his own."

Tank looked quite pleased to be chosen. "What have I got to do?"

Sunny and Blue told him to go into the barn and into the flour store. He was to look in the far corner and bring back whatever he found. Tank ran off into the barn and soon returned, holding a large, round container. He put it down onto the table and King asked Act to open it.

"Of course I will," she replied. Once opened, she looked inside the tin and brought out a beautiful cake. "That's amazing! We have never had a cake before!"

"Would you mind cutting it up into pieces so everyone can have some?" King asked Mark.

Mark took the knife and cut the cake carefully. Everyone came closer, eager for a piece of the cake, before taking it back to their place at the table. Tank couldn't wait; he ate his before he even got back to his seat.

"Yummy! It's even better in my tummy!" he announced.

Everyone laughed and before they realised it, the sun had gone down and it had started to get quite dark. Act told the children to get off to bed, and they all stood up and called out good night.

"I'll be up in a minute to tuck you in," Act said.

Blue and Sunny called out together. "We will tell you the rest of our adventures tomorrow. Good night!"

"Good night, sleep tight," King and Re-ad called out.

Stage, Act and the two dragons cleared up and soon they all went to bed, to get some much-needed sleep.

***

By the end of the first day Grambold realised that the dragons were not returning. Due to the connection between himself and the green dragon, he was sure nothing bad had happened to them; if it had he would have felt something – but he couldn't think of where they might have gone. As the hours passed and stretched into days, he began to think that they must have flown home to the farm. He decided there and then that he would make his way back there.

Chapter Twenty-Five
Grambold's Destiny

Once the family decided to stay on, life on the farm changed dramatically for the three-headed dragon. As news spread about it being such a family friendly place it soon became a busy hub, with people coming and going, all keen to barter, not just for food but with other traders.

The two dragons were very popular some visitors came just to see and talk to them, even though they were big and imposing. They towered way above everyone and their rear legs were as tall as the average man. The dragons were always the first to be seen by approaching strangers, who were never put off because of the sounds of laughter and the din of chatter that surrounded them.

Within weeks families started to build homes on the outer edges of the farm, and over time, more and more people came to settle in the surrounding areas, drawn by the security of a growing community.

King realized early on that with so many settlers arriving, there would be a greater demand for the crops and food the farm produced, so it was decided by everyone to extend the field, enabling them to grow more crops.

Both Whitestar and Trampo were put to work, pulling out tree stumps and ferrying rocks away before the ground could be ploughed ready for seeding. Stage worked side-by-side with the two dragons until the sun went down, it took several days to clear the land.

Once the extended field was ready the whole family joined in the task of sowing the seeds. Everyone held a sack of seeds over their shoulders. They all stood in a line at one end of the field, and as they walked forward together the seed was taken from each sack by hand and tossed out onto the ground. With everyone working together the task was completed by midday.

Act volunteered to make the bread, the butter and cheese. All five children wanted to be involved with the everyday tasks around the farm, so each of them were given chores to do, which were closely monitored by Act. While she appreciated her children's enthusiasm, she made sure the work was not too arduous or too tasking.

Sunny's advice to the children was simple. "Try and make a game of whatever task you're doing, that's what we did." He looked at Tank, Tim and Tame, who had been given the job of milking the cows each morning and continued "We three loved milking the cows – we would squirt the milk into the air then we tried to catch it in our mouths!"

King butted in. "There are lots of little jobs that we'll miss doing – we are quite envious of you all!"

Tank couldn't wait to try it out, so he grabbed Tim and Tame by the hands and shouted. "Come on! Let's try milking those cows now!"

Mark and Susan watched as the three disappeared into the barn and as they turned around to walk away Susan looked at the green dragon. "Are you sad because you can't do some of your old jobs?"

Sunny and Blue answered together. "No! no, there are always new things that we look forward to trying. It's important to enjoy whatever you are doing at the time, that way you won't be sad if you can no longer do those same jobs later."

The three heads looked at one another as both children walked off towards the house, Mark whistling and Susan humming the same tune. "What great kids, their parents are doing a very good job of bringing them up," King said.

Grambold had been on the long walk back to the farm, and as the weeks passed, he started to think about his own life. For the first time, he began to wonder what was his purpose in life? What was the meaning of his existence? The more he thought about it, the more vexed and troubled he became. More and more questions popped into his head and he couldn't seem to find the answers to them. Why was he doing this task? What was to become of all the information and sightings he had diligently recorded? Who would benefit from his work?

What linked him so strongly to the three-headed dragon? Was the dragon the reason he was so troubled now? So many questions were unanswered and constantly swirled around in his head.

Grambold was relieved to finally spy the farm's large barn in the distance. In a spur of the moment decision, he left the invisibility cloak in his large leather satchel. As he approached the outskirts of the farm, he was astonished to see so many new settlers in their little houses. He passed them, one after the other and was greeted with cheery smiles and waves.

For three hundred years, Grambold had not experienced any human interaction. To his surprise, he found himself eagerly waving back to the newcomers, and smiled broadly. Several children waved too, and on seeing them, he felt even better in himself. It was as if the simple act of exchanging a wave and a smile with someone else had boosted his mood. He had missed this he realized a simple gesture with so much meaning.

The farm was bustling – he had never seen so many people in one place before. It was intimidating to walk among so many strangers, but everyone was friendly, although their recognition of his presence was difficult to get used to. He'd hidden away in the shadows for such a long time, now to have people aware of his presence seemed peculiar.

He slowly walked towards where the green dragon was standing. The dragon was conducting three different conversations with three people, all at the same time. Grambold was happy to remain standing nearby, watching them and tried to hear what the three heads were talking about, although it proved impossible to follow.

Susan approached him, holding out her hand. For a moment, Grambold stared at it before he slowly took her hand in his and shook it.

"I'm Susan, welcome to the farm," she said politely. "Is there anything I can help you with?"

Grambold nodded shyly. "I was hoping to talk to the green dragon about something important."

Susan frowned, and glanced across at the three-headed dragon. "If it's important, perhaps it would be better to come back at the end of the day."

Grambold nodded in agreement. "There are so many people here and many have built homes nearby, I assume there are lots of children living around the farm now?" he asked curiously. An idea was beginning to form in his head.

"Fifteen or so, but the numbers change weekly. I have four brothers and sisters, so there's over twenty of us living on and around the farm. Why do you ask?" Susan asked politely.

Grambold thought for a minute and then surprised himself when he responded. "Well, I was thinking that perhaps with all those children, you would need a teacher. It's one of the reasons I want to speak to the green dragon."

Susan looked surprised for a moment before she nodded enthusiastically. "You definitely need to come back later, when the day's work is done and everyone has gone home. My parents will be there, as well."

Grambold smiled. "I'll come tonight," he agreed before he turned to walk away.

Susan called after him. "I am sorry, but I didn't get your name."

Grambold felt bad because he had forgotten to introduce himself. He would need to work on his social skills, now that he had decided to mix with people. He offered Susan a little bow. "Grambold!" he said. "My name is Grambold."

He stood by the wagon for quite some time and watched the scene before him. The place was buzzing with people, and the strange thing was, he felt perfectly at home here. He was sure that by teaching the children in this newly-flourishing community, he would be contributing something worthwhile. Suddenly, he began to feel very good about himself.

With plenty of time before the end of the day, Grambold decided to walk out to the edge of the field, where he settled down to wait in the shade of a tree. Thinking about his sudden announcement to Susan, he realised that if he was accepted as a teacher, it would be a major turning point in his life. Perhaps the three hundred years he'd spent watching and recording the world around him had been a prerequisite to becoming a teacher? Instead of being on the outside looking in, he would be inside, living and enjoying life with others.

Had he finally found his destiny? He really
suspected he had.

Chapter Twenty-Six
Grambold Meets the Green Dragon

Snuggling down and using the base of the tree as a pillow, Grambold nodded off to sleep and when he awoke the sun was emitting a beautiful red glow just before it started to set. "What a lovely sight," he thought to himself as he got to his feet.

A few minutes later he entered the farm yard and walked towards a long trestle table. Susan came out of the barn and called. "Grambold! You have timed your arrival perfectly, we are about to eat supper. My mother has invited you to eat with us, please come and sit here." Susan gestured to the chair nearest to the end of the table. "You'll be sitting ncxt to the green dragon. I've already told the dragons and my parents why you want to see them, they are looking forward to meeting you." She then sat down in the empty chair next to his.

Just as Grambold was about to sit down, the doors of the barn burst open. Tank hurried out, carrying a large tray of bread. Grambold rushed over to him, reached out with both arms. "Hello, please, let me help you with that."

"No, no! I can do it – besides, you are our guest; please sit down" Tank insisted.

Grambold reluctantly walked over to his seat and sat down feeling quite uncomfortable in company. Re-ad appeared with several of the children following closely behind all were carrying items of food which they placed on the table. The children sat down and Re-ad walked to the other end of the table, where she settled down so her arms were just visible above the table. The green dragon appeared a minute later with Stage and Act and the remainder of the children. They placed their items onto the table and sat down, the green dragon stretched out in the same way as Re-ad.

King turned to their guest. "Welcome, Grambold! Please don't stand on ceremony, we hate it when good food gets cold, meanwhile, let us introduce ourselves."

Grambold held a hand up in the air and looked over to Act and said graciously. "May I first thank you for your invitation to have dinner with your family which, is something I haven't done for a very long time. I am so pleased to meet you all, he then looked at them in turn bowed his head to each and rattled off all their names, including Sunny, Blue's and King's, before he calmly reached for some food and began to eat, aware that everyone around the table was watching him.

King was intrigued, and directed a question to Grambold. "That was quite an accomplishment knowing everyone's name. Do tell us how you did it?"

Grambold swallowed down a mouthful of freshly-cooked peas and glanced around the table. He cleared his throat feeling a little uncomfortable and turned towards King. "Before I reveal how I knew them, can I ask what you think of my request to teach the children in your community?"

Act stood up her expression cool. "Teachers have a role of great responsibility to fulfil. They must be totally trustworthy, and I'm afraid, Mr Grambold, that withholding secrets does not bode well towards earning such trust," She sat back down and lowered her gaze to her plate, clearly anxious about Grambold's behaviour.

Grambold rubbed his long beard nervously between his fingers, thinking about what to say. He had gotten off to a poor start, it was clear he should consider his next words carefully. He decided to tell everyone the truth about himself, before they got angry and he hurriedly rose to his feet. "I agree wholeheartedly with Act's statement about teachers, and consequently, I apologise for the way I have begun our discussion. Please, forgive me and I will tell you my secrets and how I came to know your names."

Grambold began by giving them a small insight into his life story, and what had happened to him since his discovery of the invisible cloak, three hundred years ago.

He explained about his life's work of recording not just history of their world, but also the facts and knowledge that he had found and how he hoped to pass that knowledge on, not only to the children, but also to the adults if they were interested in learning.

He said earnestly "I believe that if your community is to survive and prosper it needs to learn new skills, and the most important of those is to be able to read and write"

He reached under the table and brought out his book, opened it and then flicked a few of the pages so they could see inside, "This is my book and this is what the written word looks like."

He placed the open book down onto the table those who sat next to him peered at it. Aware that none of them had seen a book before, he invited them "Please pass it round so you can all look at it."

The book is passed around the table and he took the opportunity to eat some more food.

Explaining further "With the ability to read you would be able to attain the knowledge and skills within a books contents. Not just one skill but many. Being able to write would mean that a new skill learnt by anyone else could be recorded in another book."

King interrupted "So all the knowledge in the world could be recorded in books, that anyone could read and learn from that would be so useful. Does your book contain all the knowledge?"

"No it does not. I have over one hundred books in all and even they do not contain all the knowledge. You are a growing community your knowledge must also grow."

He concluded by telling them that some thirty years ago, he'd been drawn to a small, newly-hatched three-headed dragon, and looked towards the green dragon and said.

"I have watched you grow throughout the years, and I was present when you went off on your adventures to discover a name for King.

I was there when you learned to fly. I don't know why, but I believe our destinies are linked to one another and my part is to teach this community, so that they can all grow and prosper together." Grambold sat back down, hoping he'd made amends.

King said "Thank you for your truthfulness, you have obviously lived an extraordinarily long and interesting life.

Sunny and Blue both nodded and spoke together. "It's very strange – now that we've met you, we both feel as if we've known you all our lives, even though we've never set eyes on you before now. It seems your presence was often felt even though we weren't aware of it at the time. You have our vote to teach here." They looked at Act and Stage, and asked them "What do you think?"

Act spoke directly to Grambold. "You have led a strange, but somewhat solitary life, which probably explains why you began the way you did. Your honesty is to be commended."

Stage asked "Can writing be used for anything else?"

"It could be used as a way to communicate with one another and would allow a message to be taken from one side of Pangreat to the other. Grambold looked around the table at the children and continued "You must have made friends on your travels and have no idea how they are."

"Yes, I have made some very good friends and would love to know how they are!" Susan stated.

"Well!" Grambold said. "If you could write, you could put your words onto a parchment telling them how you are and what you have been doing and you could ask how they are."

"How would we get the parchment to my friends?" Susan asked.

"You could give it to someone who is travelling in that direction – people are always travelling from one place to another. Oak-ley uses her roots to communicate, we would be communicating too, just in a different manner—"

Blue and Sunny interrupted. "Wait! You know Oak-ley?"

"Yes," Grambold replied, he swallowed down another mouthful of food. "I met her some fifty years ago, she is a very interesting tree. You must have thought the same, because you spent a long time talking to her."

"You were there too?" King sounded surprised.

Grambold answered, a little bashful. "Yes, I was there. I was hiding in a nearby cave."

Tank had been waiting patiently for his chance to ask the big question "Please Grambold can we see your cloak?"

Grambold reached down into his bag and took out the cloak and slipped it on.

"You obviously can't see the cloak but you can see how it works" he said jokingly

"Awesome" Tank uttered" the other

children screamed with delight.

Even Tame shouted excitedly "Yes! Yes! that's great"

"Please can I try it on" Susan asked expectantly. Her eyes lit up as Grambold took it off and passed her the cloak, at the same time he looked over to Act and asked "Is that okay with you Act? " she nodded her head, and observed that he had a lovely way with children.

"You can all share the use of it" Grambold declared.

All five clustered together as Susan put on the cloak. They all ran around playing the best game of hide and seek. Each took it in turns to use the invisible cloak.

Act had made her mind up "Grambold I think you would make a very good teacher," she announced.

Stage nodded and agreed with his wife's statement. "If my wife is happy so am I, we will join you too. We can't speak for the others in the community, you must ask them yourself."

Re-ad looked as if she was about to say something, but she hesitated. King noticed and spoke up. "Have you anything to say Re-ad?"

"I was wondering what the children thought; do they want to learn about all those things?"

Stage called out "Children will you all come here please" Tame appeared from under the cloak and all five came and stood near Stage who asked them "Do you want to learn from Grambold?"

"Yes, we do!" was the resounding response from one and all.

Grambold grinned "That's great, I do hope that other grown ups will join in too. I believe I have much to offer the whole community can I have my cloak back? you can play with it another time." He took it from Tame and placed it in his bag.

King glanced up as a shooting star streaked across the sky and everyone was compelled to follow his gaze. King smiled. "It looks as if the stars think it's a good idea too." They all clapped their hands in delight.

The meal finished Act told the children. "Time for you to get off to bed, daddy and I will be in when all the clearing up is done." Obediently, the children did as they were told and said good night to everyone before disappearing into the farm house.

Grambold had been particularly affected by the children's friendliness and the warmth they'd directed towards him. "Goodnight, children!" he shouted. "I look forward to seeing you tomorrow and perhaps we could have our first lesson!" He looked across at Stage and Act, realizing that perhaps he should have gotten their permission first. "If that's all right with your parents, of course?" He was quite relieved when they both nodded their agreement.

Re-ad got to her feet. "I think it's time I got some sleep."

Sunny, Blue and King said "Goodnight Re-ad"

"Goodnight Re-ad" Grambold replied.

King then turned to Grambold. "I've just realized you have nowhere to stay. We can offer you accommodation above the horse's stable – there is a good space at the far end, which is dry and warm. Will you be able to manage with that, until we can find somewhere more suitable for you to live?"

Grambold answered with a delighted laugh. "Thank you, it will do nicely, I'm sure. I have certainly slept in worse places. No need to show me the way, I'm sure I'll find it okay." Grambold got to his feet picked up his bag and began to walk towards the stable, but he suddenly stopped and turned back, tears visible in his eyes. "Words cannot explain how happy I am, to at last have an opportunity to be a part of your life."

The three-headed dragon walked across to him and put a clawed hand on his shoulder, while Act and Stage quietly began to clear the table.

King spoke gently. "We can sense that you are a good man, someone who has been guided throughout his long life by his heart. I'm sure that is why you have been drawn to us, just as Miller was. He looked after us like sons and in return, we learned to love him like a father." King stopped abruptly as tears flowed from three sets of dragon eyes.

The older wiser Grambold cleared his throat, and spoke gently. "What a sight we are. Love is an emotion which is very powerful, tears are one of the signs of its powers."

"Grambold, we are happy that you are here with us and that you're going to stay," Sunny and Blue said together.

Grambold held their clawed hand in his. "Tomorrow is the beginning of a new chapter in my life. I look forward to the challenge." With a little spring in his step, Grambold turned and walked away. "Goodnight King, Sunny, Blue, and the same to you Act and Stage"

Sage and Act said their "Goodnight"

The three heads called out as one. "Good night!"

Chapter Twenty-Seven

Grambold's First Lesson

The following morning Susan was sent to invite Grambold to breakfast and whilst eating Grambold asked Stage "Would it be okay if I use your wagon for my lesson?"

Stage was more than happy for him to use it "You can, for as long as you need it" he replied.

King then asked Stage. "We have spent so much time on the new field we need to catch up with the work in the mill, can you give us a hand?"

Re-ad spoke before Stage could respond. "I would love to help with that."

"Thank you for the offer," Sunny and Blue said. "The problem is, even though we've got slimmer, we have grown longer and taller, so there is only enough room in the flour mill for Stage to get around with us sorry about that."

"No need to be sorry, I didn't think of that. I enjoy helping with the work and want to do whatever I can."

King looked at Re-ad and said. "Sorry but there is not much for you to do over the next few days".

"Oh, to be honest I was getting a little home sick and was wondering when I might be able to return home. If you're sure you don't need me, I could go today." Re-ad replied.

Sunny and Blue were quick to reply "We know what it's like to be home sick don't hang about go now it will do you good."

Without a second thought she turned around and called out. "Goodbye everybody." With her wings unfolding, she took off gracefully, and flew towards the three-peaked mountain. They all watched until she became a small spot in the sky and eventually disappeared.

Everyone who came to the mill that morning were informed that it would be closed at midday and told the reason why.

The family and the three headed dragon finished their work just before midday, because they were keen to attend Grambold's first lesson. The children ran and skipped over to Grambold. "Come, come, sit up on the wagon. There is room for all five of you," he said.

Quite a lot of people turned up. Word had obviously gotten around. King addressed the crowd "Good day, good day to you all and for those of you are new comers I must tell you what is happening. We have closed because we are fortunate enough to have a special teacher among us. You are welcome to join us."

A short rather gruff lady shouted out. "Most of us have been taught what we need to know by our fathers and mothers. Why do we need another teacher? What else can he teach us?"

People started to chatter noisily to one another in agreement. Stage walked forward and addressed them. "Grambold is over four hundred years old", she paused as a hush descended over the crowd. It was apparent none of them had ever seen anyone of that age before.

She looked around at the crowd raised her right hand and pointed with her finger and said. "We all respect our elders for their wisdom and their knowledge." She stopped and put her arm down to her side. "We need to learn all we can from this man" she pointed towards Grambold "That is why I want him to teach us and our children. I will now let him tell you what he can teach us and why." Stage stepped back everyone was quiet.

Grambold in a steady calm voice said, "I have come across many other communities in my time unfortunately most of them have not survived. Do you want this to happen here?"

Some shook their heads others called out "No!"

Grambold continued "Good we all have a common goal the life and prosperity of this community." Many nodded and agreed between each other.

"There is wisdom in the ladies words but being taught by your parent means you have not learnt anything new. For the community to prosper and to keep growing many of you will need additional new skills."

He took out of his pocket a piece of white soft stone and started to make marks on the barn wall and said "These markings represent the spoken word it's called writing" He stopped and turned around.

A tall young man called out "I can not hear them can anyone else?"

Of course no one can, there was lots of laughter as people saw the funny side of the comment.

The same young man asked "What do those markings say?"

Grambold smiled and said "I will read what these words say." He pointed his finger at the first word and moved along pointing at each word in turn. He spoke slowly. "This is your first step to great knowledge."

He turned to face the crowd and said "The skills in writing and reading will equip you with the tools to be more intelligent. The born leaders amongst you will also benefit from this skill."

An older man called out "Will we all need to learn this reading and writing?"

Grambold replied "No! only those who wish to. Mothers and fathers should decide if they want their children to have these lessons. Don't worry I have many other things to teach you."

Grambold produced an old pigs bladder that he had prepared earlier. It was the only thing he could find that was round. Holding it high in the air he then said. "This resembles the shape of our world, I know you all believe it's flat but I am here to tell you that it's round."

He drew a picture of the world on the barn wall. Everyone was fascinated. His illustration showed the outline of Pangreat and the sea surrounding it and the location of the sun, he told them "The earth travels around the sun like this" showing it on his drawing.

When he finished speaking, some people seemed surprised by what they had heard and seen, they talked to one another in hushed tones. Grambold was anxious regarding how his lesson had been received. "If you have no questions, that will be all for today. I will be here again at the same time tomorrow. Thank you for joining us."

He climbed down from the wagon several people closest to him rushed up to him and individuals started shaking his hand congratulating him. One said "Thank you that was very interesting I'll be back tomorrow."

Another took his hand and said "Yes it was good I will be back too."

A line of people waited to speak to him. Grambold was a little overwhelmed by all the positive responses, several parents called out "We and our children will be here tomorrow."

The green dragon was pleased that it all went so well for Grambold. Sunny and Blue called out "Well done Grambold."

King also shouted "Grambold that was very good."

Sunny and Blue announced "We will be opening the mill and farm shortly."

Two days later Re-ad returned to the farm. As she approached the barn she noticed a large gathering of people around the wagon, all seemed to be listening intently to what Grambold was saying. She was pleased to see that Grambold's lessons were being well received and she landed some way from the group.

The green dragon walked over to Re-ad and King asked "Hi did the trip home go well, are you feeling better?"

She looked happier and said "Yes it did go well and I feel a lot better, thank you for asking. Things seem to be going well here."

Sunny and Blue replied "Yes it's really good, everyone seems to be benefiting from the lessons we learn something new each day."

King said "We have always been quick learners reading seems to be easy for us but we are finding writing difficult, our fingers and claws are so big. The feathers that Grambold gives us to write with are very flimsy."

Sunny and Blue added "We are better writing on the barn wall using a soft white stone. It's not very practical but Grambold told us it didn't matter, at least we are getting some practice."

"I can't wait to join you" Re-ad said eagerly.

Chapter Twenty-Eight
Susan's Adventure

Several months had passed and the community around Miller's Farm had grown to over one hundred and fifty. More houses had been built, all had good size plots of land so the occupants could either keep live stock or grow food for themselves.

Silly arguments started to flare up which led to disputes. Those involved took the disputes to the two dragons to resolve them. After overseeing several disputes both dragons decided that a better course of action was needed.

Grambold was consulted by the dragons and he advised them saying. "The community needs to get together and elect some leaders. These leaders can then help resolve any disputes. "These are good people and they already know the meaning of right and wrong they just need reminding and a little help to keep them on the straight and narrow."

One morning at the breakfast table, King couldn't help but notice that Re-ad seemed unusually quiet and asked tenderly. "Are you all right you look sad are you feeling a little home sick?"

She replied."You know me so well even though I think of this place as my home, it's been months since I last visited my cave."

King smiled and said. "You are silly why didn't you mention it before? Look its going to be quiet here over the next few days why don't you go today? You could leave straight away."

Susan who had been listening to the conversation piped up. "Oh ! mother do you think I could go with Re-ad this time. I would love to see her cave she has told me so much about it."

Act looked around the table she had always been happy to allow the children to ride on the dragon's backs, so she nodded her approval. "Okay you can go but you must do what ever Re-ad tells you."

Susan ran around the table and gave her mother a hug and kiss. "Thank you so much mummy," she turned to Re-ad and asked, "When are we going?"

Re-ad smiled and replied. "I hadn't really decided to go, but I can't disappoint you now."

Act rushed off to the farm house and called out "I'll get something for you to eat and drink," she returned with a bulging leather carry sack which she handed to her daughter.

Susan threw it over her shoulder "Thanks mummy" at the same time Act gave her a hug.

Stage and all the other children were keen to hug Susan, each said their "Goodbyes." She then expertly climbed onto Re-ad's back, and held tight onto the leather strap that had been secured in place by Re-ad.

Re-ad walked forward her wings came out and they were airborne in seconds. Susan called out "Bye" and waved with her free hand. Everyone around the farm waved as they flew off.

Re-ad instinctively headed in the direction of the three peaked mountain. The two of them became a small spot in the sky and soon disappeared out of view. Re-ad climbed higher and higher. After an hour she called out to Susan. "Are you all right?"

Susan's teeth were chattering and answered, "I'm just a little cold."

Re-ad heard a small tremor in Susan's voice, "You poor thing" she said sympathetically and she made a quick descent.

Re-ad explained. "We were quite high up that's why you felt cold, but now that we are lower you will warm up."

Chapter Twenty-Nine

Unseen Danger

It was way past midday when Re-ad brought them down to land just short of her cave.

Susan climbed down and started to run towards the entrance. "Oh I can't wait to see inside" she said excitedly.

Re-ad shouted in a commanding voice "Stop! Susan stop!" Susan instantly came to a stop just outside the entrance. She had a worried look on her face she'd never heard Re-ad shout so sternly before.

"Come away from the entrance walk slowly!" Re-ad said in a firm voice. Susan obeyed

Re-ad quickly stepped in between Susan and the cave. She faced the opening and in a whisper said "Something is not right here it smells all wrong."

Re-ad sniffed the air and then the ground without turning around she said quietly "Move further away!"

Again Susan obeyed. Re-ad quickly turned away rushed towards Susan then grabbed hold of her and placed her onto her back saying. "Hold on very tight."

Suddenly they were airborne again Re-ad climbed up and away from the cave, as fast as she could, Susan held on very tightly with both hands.

She couldn't stop herself from looking back towards the cave just as two brown and yellow giant snakes slithered out of the entrance. Their forked tongues darted in and out of their large teeth lined mouths. Two pairs of black eyes stared up at them. Both monsters heads rose up from the ground suspended by their thick round long bodies, their mouths opened widely.

Snakes

Susan was sure that they would actually reach up and snatch them out of the sky.

Re-ad is far too high for them to be in any danger. The two snakes seemed to follow them for some way. Susan called out "I'll keep watching out for them you just concentrate on getting us to safety."

Re-ad flew at a tremendous speed following the valley. At the mouth of the valley she suddenly turned sharp left, in an effort to lose the snakes and headed towards another mountain in the distance. She circled around the side of the mountain and landed half way up telling Susan in a calm voice "You can get down now. I am sorry if I scared you but as you saw those snakes are very big and dangerous especially to someone your size"

Susan had a glazed look in her eyes that Re-ad had never seen before. Then Susan started to talk incessantly. "I was scared at first when you told me to stop. I was so surprised when you suddenly snatched me up. I thought I was going to die when the snakes reached up to try and grab me off your back. We were flying so fast and close to the mountains I was sure we were going to crash into them. It was a good job I was holding on tight otherwise I would have fallen off when you made that sharp turn."

Re-ad placed her clawed hand to Susan's face and gently touched her lips with a finger and said quietly "Shush you were very brave but now you need to stop talking and start to calm down, breathe slowly."

Susan took comfort from the gesture and the soft spoken words. She started to breathe slower and calmed down.

"We'll be safe here for a while. I don't want to put you in any more danger. If I had the energy and the strength to fly us back now I would but it's also too late anyway." She looked around as if she was searching for something and said almost in a whisper "I need to breathe fire to make sure we stay safe."

Re-ad stopped bent down and removed some dead branches to one side. In another whisper said "Here's the oil I was looking for," she drank some and led Susan into a small hollow nearby. She sniffed the ground her head suddenly disappeared into a hole. She withdrew her head and whispered, "That's enough gas, it's been some time since I've done all this, come with me just a little further."

Susan walked beside Re-ad up the side of the mountain where Re-ad eventually stopped and reached into a small crack and pulled out some sparklight. She placed it between her teeth, and whispered, "That's it I will be able to keep us safer now that I can breathe fire."

Susan asked in a whisper "Why are you whispering?"

Re-ad answered "The sound from up here travels a long way I do not want to give our location away to those snakes."

Susan nodded her head mouthing "Okay."

Most of the fear within Re-ad seemed to have disappeared she was now far more confident. She was afraid for Susan not herself, she whispered her plan to Susan. "The best thing we can do is stay here until it starts to get dark. Then we'll fly to the coast, we can spend the night on the beach and fly back to the farm in the morning."

Chapter Thirty

Fight To The Death

What was left of the afternoon went by slowly and in silence. Re-ad constantly looked for the snakes to ensure they had not followed them.

When it was time to go and without making any undue sound Susan climbed onto Re-ad's back. Re-ad took off heading towards the beach. She landed on the sand and took up a position by the seas edge. Re-ad thought "It's a good location."

Before laying down she whispered "I want you to stay on my back all night you'll be safer there." Slowly Re-ad curled herself around and lay down so that her head was facing straight across the beach in the direction of the grassy dunes.

Once settled she turned her head from side to side checking along the beach. She whispered "We have a very good view of everything from here. It might be a good idea if you have some food now."

Susan whispered her reply "I think you should have most of it I'm not hungry." Susan opened the sack and tried to pass Re-ad most of the food.

Re-ad waved it away with her clawed hand.

Susan pulled a stern face and whispered "You need it more than me you have to fly us home tomorrow honestly I'm not hungry, but to please you I'll have some bread and cheese now take this."

Re-ad reluctantly took what had been offered, both ate in silence. Re-ad constantly scanned the stretch of beach and the sand dunes in front of them, until the last remnants of the sun disappeared below the horizon.

Re-ad whispered "Try and get some sleep I will stay awake all night to keep watch."

Susan quietly asked. "Will you wake me if you need some sleep? I can keep watch whilst you sleep."

Re-ad said "I will!" but had no intention of sleeping.

Re-ad stayed alert and awake all night. The full moon had offered some light to see with, she saw smelt or heard nothing. Dawn broke and the sun slowly rose and with it the light.

Re-ad tried to wake Susan gently but she was startled when she opened her eyes. Not because of Re-ad but from the fear that remained within her from the previous day. Re-ad reassured her with soft comforting words, "You're okay I'm here" Re-ad was distracted from her task. Suddenly a large snake appeared from out of the sand just beside them.

It tried to wrap it's self around Re-ad but she was far too strong. Re-ad, using her wings, pushed herself up onto her rear legs and in an instant flames shot out of her mouth, part of the snakes body was alight and it quickly slithered off into the sea which doused the flames. It decided to stay well away trying to cool off.

Fight with the Snake

Susan, who had been laying flat against Re-ad holding on for dear life, had seen the burning snake slither off and sat upright. She screamed out as the other snake tried to pull her off Re-ads back by wrapping its tail around her body. Susan was unable to hold on to the leather straps and was pulled off Re-ad's back, she was being wrapped tightly in several more coils of the snakes tail.

Re-ad stamped on the snakes head who she believed was holding Susan in a death grip. Re-ad shot flames over its head and instinctively bit into the rear of the snakes burning head. It stopped wriggling.

Susan was instantly dropped onto the sand gasping for breath holding her tummy and chest. The snake in the sea must have watched the demise of the other snake and slithered off along the coast as fast as it could and was not seen again.

Re-ad rushed over to where Susan was laying and in a worried tone asked "Susan are you alright?"

"Yes! Now that I can breathe. I was so frightened, have you killed the snake?" She asked.

Re-ad looked down at the sand and said sadly, "Yes I believe I did but I took no pleasure in it, the snakes were just after food. I had to do it. I was sure he was going to kill you. In the past when I lived on my own I rarely needed to kill anything for food. Most of the meat I ate came from other animals kills. I hope you didn't see what I did."

Susan looked up at Re-ad and answered truthfully "No I didn't I was too busy trying to get free. Thank you for saving my life. Can we start back to the farm now?"

"Sorry Susan I don't think I can fly us back this morning I need some food to top up my energy reserves to fly. The fight seems to have sapped me of the little strength I had." Re-ad slumped onto the sand with exhaustion. Susan rushed to her head and cradled it in her arms.

"No! don't be sorry I should have thought." Susan was concerned about Re-ad

Re-ad replied. "Let me rest a while we will be safe now, the other snake will not come back." After an hour Re-ad stood up.

They walked a little, Re-ad started to get stronger. It was not long before Re-ad made Susan climb onto her back and they flew up into the morning sky, staying low she circled around the mountain and headed up the valley.

They soon landed outside her cave Re-ad told Susan "Stay outside until I check it out. I have to be sure it's safe I can't smell anything I'll only be a few minutes you will be safe here stay in the shadows and keep still and quiet."

Re-ad entered the cave and Susan could be heard to say "Be careful Re-ad."

"I will" replied Re-ad as she disappeared into the cave.

Susan stayed in the shadows for what seemed like ages, but in fact was only about five minutes. Re-ad appeared at the cave entrance, she beckoned Susan to her. "Come it's safe I have even got us some food. I will cook it and you can join me in an early morning meal."

Susan entered the tunnel that led to the large cave and said to Re-ad, "Your description of the walls did not do this place justice," and when she finally entered the main chamber her mouth fell open in amazement adding, "Re-ad this place is so beautiful the light, the colours. How you must have missed all of this."

Re-ad sighed "For the last few years it seemed to have lost most of its charms but, since I have been away I have realised how much I love the place. When I lived here with my mother we spent every day outside flying around. When she died I searched endlessly for other dragons but, I always came back every night to sleep."

In between the talking Re-ad managed to breathe fire gently onto the meat which she had placed on a large golden plate. It was now well cooked the smell in the cave made Susan realise that she too was hungry.

Re-ad laid down on the floor and Susan snuggled into her tummy both ate their fill of the meat and soon both were fast asleep.

Susan woke up it seemed lighter in the cave it was as if someone had shone a light into her eyes. She called "Re-ad wake up! wake up!"

Re-ad woke and both of them walked outside to see the sun directly over head it was midday.

"That was just what I needed" Re-ad said "Let's get going" she concluded.

Susan quickly climbed onto Re-ad's back and they were soon flying high over the dazzling blue sea and well on their way. A slight wind came from behind them which helped them get home much quicker than when they flew out.

Chapter Thirty-One
Home Safe

As they came down to land the whole family including the green dragon could be seen on the ground ready to greet and welcome them home.

Re-ad stood back whilst Susan was hugged and kissed by her family everyone was glad to see her. King sensed that something was wrong.

Re-ad stepped forward and asked Stage and Act "Please can you two join me in the barn I have something to tell you."

Susan knew what Re-ad wanted them for and said. "I need to be there but without my brothers and sisters."

Stage and Act both sensed there was something wrong. They behaved calmly as if there was nothing the matter, Stage told the children "Okay go and do some of your chores we'll see you later."

Stage, Act and Susan walked into the barn. Ra-ad was the last to enter. King went to whisper something to her, but Re-ad told him abruptly "Please stay out side and listen to what is being said."

Re-ad closed the barn door behind her and stood in front of the three of them Susan was standing in between her parents. Re-ad looked down at the floor feeling very guilty. She then looked up at Stage and towards Act and said in nothing more than a whisper.

"Please don't interrupt me whilst I am telling you what has happened. If you stop me I don't think I could go on" She took a big breath and continued "I am so sorry but I put Susan in terrible danger by taking her with me."

They could see little tears in her eyes. Stage and Act looked at her tenderly and she was able to go on. Both parents found it hard to listen without interrupting but bit their tongues and waited until Re-ad had finished talking.

The initial shock that Stage and Act first experienced seemed to wear off, it was obvious that Susan was unharmed and back with them safe and sound.

Susan stepped closer to Re-ad and said to her parents. "What she failed to tell you was, she did everything in her power to keep me safe. First by stopping me from going in the cave. Second on the beach she stayed awake all night. Then in the morning when the snakes attacked us she saved my life. She saw one off after setting him alight. He disappeared into the sea. She was then forced to kill the other snake because it was squeezing the life out of me."

Stage and Act were visibly shocked. Susan realised that she should not have told her parents so many details.

Re-ad commented "You have one very brave daughter."

"I felt braver the closer I got to all those I love. You were right Re-ad those snakes were doing what came naturally. I also feel sorry that you had to kill one of them but I am glad it was him and not me." Susan replied.

Re-ad spoke tenderly "I am so glad you are alright I was concerned for your safety."

Re-ad suddenly sank down onto the floor, Susan was the first to reach her and held her head in her arms. Stage and Act rushed over.

Stage knowingly said "It's shock linked with feelings of total relief."

The doors opened suddenly as the green dragon hurried in, he had heard the thud on the floor and came in to find out what it was, seeing Re-ad on the floor he rushed to her side.

King said full of concern "Re-ad are you okay?"

"You're going to be okay just breathe slowly." Sunny and Blue said together.

Re-ad looked around at everyone and in a small voice said shyly. "I'm alright, please can you help me up." The green dragon helped her to stand.

Once she had stood up she responded with "There I feel fine" but her first few steps were a bit wobbly. The green dragon had a good hold of her. When outside she was able to walk unaided. The strength had come back to her legs.

That night the story is related to the whole family. Grambold entered it into his book.

Later in the evening Re-ad got rid of the gas and oil and placed the sparklight on one of the old walls outside the barn.

Within a few days everything is back to normal on the farm. The community grow by another small family. They started to build their home further afield because the area was getting too congested.

Chapter Thirty-Two
The Evil Side of Nature

Meanwhile on the far side of Pangreat lived a flock of Manhawks who were created by nature a long time ago, as a balance to all the good in the world.

They lived in caves set inside the ridge of a crumbled old volcano which was completely surrounded by a petrified forest. Animals came from miles around attracted by the mosses and algae that grew abundantly on the trees, it was a nourishing and much needed food source for them.

These Manhawks as the name suggests are a strange mixture of humans and hawks. The neck, body, arms hands and legs down to the knee joint are human. The lower legs are covered with small feathers culminating in hawk taloned claws.

Their cheeks, chin, mouth, teeth, tongue and beaked shaped nose are human. The eye sockets hold orange and black hawk-like eyes and eye lids to match.

Small feathers grow from their eyebrow line and cover the hawk shaped skull, with its hidden hawk-type ears. The skull contains a tiny divided brain, which is also part hawk and part human.

Feathered wings grow in between the shoulder blades, but they are small in comparison to the body and this is one of the reasons they cannot fly – along with the fact that they haven't got a tail.

Animal furs were used by the Manhawks as their only form of clothing, with the men wearing the furs as shorts-type garments, and the females wearing them similarly, but with extra strips of fur covering their torsos.

The Manhawks made spears, bows and arrows, and wooden clubs that they used to hunt and fight with. Hunting parties would lay in wait up in the trees to ambush their prey. Their small wings just allowed them to glide down, silently and deadly.

Manhawk

Strict rules and a pecking order of authority had been in place within the flock for generations. Lower ranking Manhawks who were born with a much smaller human part of the brain, were expected to do the hunting and all the work – they got beaten if they failed in their tasks, or were too slow to finish them.

No one not even Oak-ley were aware of the evil plot which had been hatched some five years earlier.

It came about when a challenger named Bravehawk won his place as the new leader. He was sly and very clever and was instrumental in the death of the old leader, making it look like an accident.

Once in power he moved quickly and took a top ranking female named Shreakhawk for his mate.

He decreed that all paired Manhawks were to start producing eggs; only Shreakhawk knew his true plans and together they encouraged the breeding.

Bravehawk told Shreakhawk a story about a flying horse with its magical horn. He believed the horn gave the flying horse the ability to fly. Bravehawk told her he wanted to steal the magical horn. He had convinced himself that if he ground it down into dust and ate some, he would gain the ability to fly, something he always wanted to do.

Within those five years the flock had produced eighteen new Manhawks. Three were Bravehawk's sons – because Manhawks only live for sixty years, Bravehawk wanted to achieve his goal before he got much older. So he and Shreakhawk started to make their plans. Their three offspring would not be part of the plan it was considered to be a menial task like hunting, not fit for high birth Manhawks so they needed someone else to lead the fifteen.

Shreakhawk had heard of a yearling one of the fifteen,who was very clever she invited the youngster to meet Bravehawk.

Bravehawk who was sitting in the leader's throne asked her. "Why is this yearling here?"

"This is Featherhawk, I told him to come because he could be the solution to our problem."

"How can that be?" Bravehawk questioned.

"Firstly he is not high born, he is clever with, according to his mother, superior mental abilities, he has proven to be one of our best hunters and a natural leader of the hunting parties. May I ask Featherhawk some questions?" Shreakhawk asked, looking towards Bravehawk for his permission.

Bravehawk grew impatient and snarled at her. "Get on with it!"

She walked closer to Featherhawk and asked him"Why are you such a good hunter?"

Featherhawk looked surprised for a moment, before he spoke. "I plan the hunt before we start"

"Can you give an example of a plan?" Shreakhawk asked.

Much to Bravehawk's surprise, the yearling gave a detailed step by step plan of a typical hunt down to the positioning of every hunter, he even highlighted each individual hunters weakness and strengths. It was indeed a remarkable gift for a Manhawk, something Bravehawk had never heard of before.

Bravehawk got up and approached Featherhawk, grabbed him by the hand and shook it firmly. He drew the yearling into a hug with his other arm and whispered in his ear. "I have a proposition for you. Would you like to be promoted to the highest rank in the flock? Answerable only to Shreakhawk and me?"

Featherhawk nodded his head and stuttered out a response."Y— yes, yes I, I would."

Bravehawk continued. "Good. We have a special role that only you can carry out. We want you to lead fourteen Manhawks on a hunt to find a flying horse with a single magical horn growing out of its head. I want you to bring that horn back to me. Will you do it?"

Featherhawk answered instantly, and

nodded in agreement. "Yes, I will."

Bravehawk pulled away. "It's settled then. Go now and tell your parents about your new position. Be ready in the morning to lead the fourteen"

The following day, the whole flock were assembled to say goodbye to the fifteen

Bravehawk stood before them and spoke. "Featherhawk will lead you on this hunt to seek out a flying horse he knows the plan and once you are on the way he will instruct you on the task ahead. Travel towards where the sun rises every day, that should lead you in the right direction." With Featherhawk leading the group, their long journey began.

Chapter Thirty-Three
The Manhawks Rampage

Bravehawk had no idea how the group were getting on he found this most disconcerting. He didn't know that Featherhawk was proving to be an excellent leader of the group.

Featherhawk soon realised that the old way of hunting was too time consuming and not very practical. He instigated a better system of tracking whilst also searching for the Unicorns.

A daily routine had developed, starting first thing in the morning two or three Manhawks were sent out ahead of the main group to hunt and scout. This proved to be very successful for the first few weeks, unfortunately with abundant prey about many animals were killed needlessly.

As the supply of prey seemed to be getting more scarce, a new strategy was implemented. Featherhawk sent groups of two or three to fan out some distance from both sides of the main group as it continued moving forward. For a while this strategy worked well.

One of these pairs of Manhawks discovered an entrance to a large cave. They ventured inside slipped and fell over the slimy smelly surface, they heard rustling sounds coming from the rear of the cave. The sound came closer, several pairs of red eyes could be seen hovering towards them. Three giant bats were flitting around them. The Manhawks began to swing their clubs thrashing wildly at the bats but the bats were too fast and dodged them easily.

A high pitched voice came from inside the cave.

"Stop, stop." The Manhawks didn't know who the voice was shouting at, they stopped thrashing out anyway, both looked into the cave. The three bats flew back into the cave and disappeared out of sight.

The voice continued. "Who are you? and what do you want?"

The male Manhawk replied. "I am Brownhawk and this is my mate Sharphawk. We are looking for a friend of ours."

"A friend you say, tell me who!" the voice seemed closer, two red eyes could now be seen in the darkness.

"A flying horse have you seen him?"Brownhawk answered.

The voice was coming from a much larger bat than the three that hovered around them. The Manhawks could see her large black furry body, rubbery looking wings were partly folded away. Her head was shaped like a massive pear with a piggy shaped nose, and within her mouth could be seen sharp white thin teeth. She had very small red dots for eyes. Two very small ears were just visible and shaped like curled up leaves, with a long antennae sticking out from behind each one.

Queen of the Bats

The voice spoke again "I am Queen of the bats, we have never seen a flying horse only jumping horns."

"Thank you," Sharphawk replied. She glanced out of the cave and turned back to face the Queen bat and then carried on speaking "It's starting to get dark out side can we spend the night in your cave?"

The Queen of the bats replied "You are more than welcome to stay, you will have the cave to yourselves. We will be going out hunting all night and won't return until just before the sun comes up."

"What will you be hunting?"Brownhawk asked.

The Queen answered "Fruit off the trees in the forest."

Suddenly there was a loud rustling sound as all the bats started to fly out of the cave. The two Manhawks dived down onto the floor of the cave anxious to get out of the way. The last to leave was the Queen who just managed to pass over them, her feet stepped on them lightly as she said. "Go further in where there is more room you'll be out of the way when we come back, sleep well," then she flew out into the dusk.

The two Manhawks slept but awoke before the bats returned. They left the cave and climbed up its face and managed to cling to the top of the entrance with their taloned feet and hands and waited for the bats.

The Queen arrived first and did not see the Manhawks as she entered the cave the others followed her. A few stragglers came along later, both Manhawks swung down hanging by their talons and managed to grab several bats each, they dropped to the ground turning in the air and landed on their clawed feet. Dispatching the bats they started to eat as they made their way eagerly to catch up with the remainder of the group to share the food.

A few days later a different pair of Manhawks came across three one metre tall giant snails. They didn't consider eating them because of the silvery slime that came from them. The male Manhawk used his club and banged on the side of the huge shell. "Have you seen a flying horse" he demanded, then said to his mate "We are not going to get anything from these dumb snails they have no brains." He killed two of the snails and the female killed the other one.

"Let's get away from all this slime" he called out.

He started to slip and ended up sprawled flat out on the slimy ground. The female tried to help him up but, she went over head first falling on top of him. He thumped her hard and managed to scramble over her. He stood up and hurried away, leaving her to get up herself.

Giant Snails

On another day three Manhawks spied the nest of an Eaggon which was perched on a very tall tree top.

Eaggons are part eagle and part dragon. They have the head of a dragon with a beak not a mouth, over lapping scales cover their head and necks. Their bodies legs and claws are the same as an eagle's so are the tails and the wings, they do not breathe fire.

Eaggon

Stealthhawk was accompanied by two females, Slimhawk and Leanhawk he looked towards them and said "We will all eat well tonight follow me."

Slowly and stealthily so as not to draw the attention of the Eaggons they started to climb the tree. It took quite a time before they reached the nest, Stealthhawk was well hidden and waited patiently for the Eaggon to leave the nest.

He didn't have to wait too long, before the female Eaggon flew off. Stealthhawk and Slimhawk climbed in to the nest and the chicks started squawking, Stealthhawk advanced towards one with his club held high. Just then the male Eaggon returned to the nest and saw what was happening.

"Stop!" he called out swooped down and snatched Stealthhawk out of the nest, as he flew up and away he plucked the wings off Stealthhawk and dropped him. Stealthhawk fell like a stone and was killed instantly when he hit the ground.

Slimhawk had seen the demise of Stealthhawk and hurried out of the nest. She started to climb down and called to Leanhawk "Get down as fast as you can"

Leanhawk panicked and jumped onto a branch that broke. She fell awkwardly and hit her head she tumbled unconscious all the way to the bottom. She was dead before she hit the ground. Slimhawk managed to get down safely and ran away as fast as she could. She did not stop until she reached the main group.

Featherhawk asked her "What has happened to the other two you were with?"

She told him what had happened, he informed them all "Stay well away from Eaggons in the future."

A few days later a pair of Manhawks were stalking a small deer. The female Treehawk said to the male Tanderhawk "I am very tired and need to stop and rest, you go on and come back for me later."

What they didn't know was that they themselves were being hunted, by a male sabre toothed tiger. He had been stalking them for sometime, he walked slowly and quietly taking one step at a time silently creeping along staying very low without being noticed the way cats do.

The tiger watched as Tanderhawk disappeared in to the trees and Treehawk lay down on the ground. The tiger moved towards her, she had no idea that he was there she drifted off to sleep. She never woke up. The final spring from the tiger enabled him to put his full weight onto his front paws and landed directly onto her fragile head which broke like an egg, she died instantly. The tiger picked up Treehawk in his mouth and carried her away.

A short while later Tanderhawk came back to where he had left Treehawk. He had not been successful with his hunt and saw a small pool of blood where Treehawk had slept. He started to follow the obvious trail left by the sabre toothed tiger not knowing what had made it or where it was leading to.

The sabre tooth tiger was a father of two cubs and he'd been hunting to feed them. As he approached the site where his mate and cubs were waiting for him he growled. His mate on hearing his roar came to greet him as she always did when she smelt food.

Tanderhawk was not far behind the male tiger when the female tiger saw him. She instinctively headed out at an angle away from her cubs. She circled around her mate as he continued walking towards the cubs who were laying perfectly still in the very long grass. Tanderhawk didn't realise the danger he was in until it was too late. The female tiger gave chase.

Tanderhawk saw her coming and turned to run, but the tiger was already at full speed and her giant strides meant that she was upon him before he took two steps. She pounced onto his back and the impact flattened him to the ground. His chest was crushed and his head hit a rock, killing him instantly.

After a few days Featherhawk realised that Tanderhawk and Treehawk were not coming back. He was sure that they had met a similar fate as Stealthhawk and Leanhawk. He spent time thinking what to do and decided that it was too dangerous to hunt in the mornings. The daily routine was changed again and he informed the group "I will lead us off early every morning and then in the afternoon I will take five of you hunting." He hoped there would be fewer predators around then.

Chapter Thirty Four
A Friend in Trouble

Oak-ley heard about the animals being killed almost immediately after the Manhawks started on their journey. Even though they came from the other side of Pangreat the thoughts reached her very quickly, flashing through the roots like an electric current. As the weeks went by she became more and more concerned. She had never known of so many animal deaths in all her life and it upset her very much.

She pondered and wondered what could be causing so much mayhem. Then she translated a word that she kept hearing. Birdmen she concluded that it meant Manhawks. Who! it seemed kept asking about a flying horse. "Unicorn Pegasus" she thought to herself. She was not unduly worried about the Unicorns because of the great distance involved. What she was concerned about was the numbers of the animals that were in immediate danger. All the deaths she had been told about was proof of that.

What could she do to help? The fairies would be visiting her within the week so before then she was hoping to have some kind of plan.

"The green dragon needed to be informed" she thought to herself. Hopefully he would know what to do. She concentrated on ways to get in touch with them. She knew he lived by the three peaked mountain. How could she send a message to him? Could the fairies fly that far? What about the badger or the fox, the birds "Oh dear!" she thought out loud. I need to think of a way to contact him.

The fairies were due in a day or two and she still hadn't thought of a way to contact the green dragon. It was all she could think of as she heard of more and more deaths.

What she didn't know was both Re-ad and the green dragon were planning to visit her the same day that the fairies were due.

King, Blue and Sunny had been able to convince Stage and Act that after such a terrible experience with the snakes, Susan needed something really special to help her get over her ordeal. Meeting Oak-ley and especially the fairies would definitely help.

Both parents took some persuading, what finally convinced them to let her go was that one of them would accompany her. Act decided that she would go. She made the case that she would worry the most, but Susan was sure it was because she wanted to meet the fairies too.

The plan was to fly out the same morning as the fairies were due to see Oak-ley. They would stay overnight in the cave that Grambold mentioned. Susan would also spend the following day with the fairies and come back the next day. Everyone thought it was a good plan. Act made up food hampers for everyone to last for three days.

Re-ad and the green dragon made harnesses for each other to carry the food and the water.

After breakfast on the morning they were due to leave, the whole community came to Millers Farm to wave them off. Susan and Act put on several layers of clothing to keep them warm. Act even had to admit to being excited, Susan and Act were kissed and hugged by the family. Susan climbed onto the green dragon's back and Act got onto Re-ad's back.

Stage stood between both dragons looked at them in turn and stated. "Look after my treasures" He then called to Act and Susan. "You two have an enjoyable time I love you both."

As both dragons took off Grambold walked over to Stage and said. "They are in good hands I'm not sure about us how is your cooking?"

Stage waved to Susan and Act. He turned around and couldn't help but laugh at Grambold's comment. "Well!" he said "You'll have to give me a hand, then you can't blame me for the bad cooking." Both men walked off laughing even louder.

The atmosphere around the farm was rather subdued. Some people drifted off home only a few new comers bothered to stay and barter for flour. At midday the farm was closed. Stage and the four children joined others for Grambold's lesson.

Several parents who had not been before came along with their children. Grambold welcomed them and asked them their names. He wrote their names down. One of the fathers asked, "What did you just do?"

Grambold replied. "I have written your names down with all the rest would you like to see it?"

Grambold walked over to the man with the parchment in his hand he pointed to his name saying. "There is your name, Goodhead would you like to learn how to write it yourself?"

Goodhead replied almost instantly "I would"

Grambold turned away and asked, "Who else would like to learn to write their name?" Half the class put their hands up some newer pupils called out "We do."

A tall lean boy stood up and said "Mr Grambold you taught some of us how to do that last time. What can we do?"

"Of course I did" said Grambold "I am sure that some of you think that teaching is easy" Grambold looked around the class there were lots of nodding heads he continued. "Okay! so today you can help teach those who can't write their names. Are you willing to do that?"

There was a resounding "Yes yes!"

Grambold paired them up, those who couldn't write with those who could, the few who were left he started to teach himself. He looked up and said loudly, "What are you waiting for? Get on with it." When the lesson had finished there were proud pupils who could now write their names, and a similar number who were doubly proud for teaching them.

Chapter Thirty-Five
Oak-ley Is Relieved

The two dragons stayed air born high in the sky for several hours. The head wind was very strong and it took longer than they thought. When they saw Re-ad's snow peaked mountain in the distance, they veered left in the general direction of the woods where Oak-ley lived.

Eventually with the green dragon in the lead they started to descend. King shouted to Re-ad over the sound of the wind, "We will land just before the forest follow me."

They came down to land just in front of Oak-ley she was so surprised. She called out excitedly.

"Thank goodness you are here I have never been so relieved to see anybody in all my life."

King said softly, "Hello Oak-ley can I introduce the young lady on my back her name is Susan, this is Oak-ley."

"Hello Oak-ley I'm so glad to meet you at last." Susan said

Oak-ley replied in her deep rich voice. "What a beautiful young lady you are and so polite."

Sunny and Blue had to get in on the act and both said together, "We know that you have seen the red dragon flying overhead this is she Re-ad."

Re-ad was genuinely happy to meet Oak-ley "I have heard a lot about you Oak-ley I can't believe how many times I have flown over this place and never once saw you."

Oak-ley replied. "Fate is a strange thing, it's good to meet you at last."

Sunny and Blue were thinking to one another about introducing Act, who had eagerly climbed down from Re-ad but she quickly introduced herself.

"Hello Oak-ley I am Susan's mother my name is Act you are the most wonderful oak tree I have ever seen I am delighted to meet you. King has told us a lot about you."

Oak-ley looked at the green dragon and said. "King! I don't know any King"

Sunny and Blue both spoke together "No name found a name it's King!"

Oak-ley looked at King and replied "It certainly suits you."

King said to Oak-ley "Susan is really looking forward to meeting the fairies are they here?"

Oak-ley whispered. "When they heard you coming the two of them hid in my branches they will come out once they realise who you are."

Just then Red Tip and Yellow Tip flew out of Oak-ley's branches Red Tip landed on King's head and Yellow Tip landed on Sunny's head.

King spoke softly "Hello Redtip this is Susan and her mother Act."

Red Tip was shy but Susan whispered, "Hello Red Tip you look so beautiful."

Red Tip giggled placing her small hand on her mouth.

Yellow Tip fluttered over and said "Hello Susan do you think I am beautiful too?"

Susan was tickled pink and remarked. "I love you both you are two absolute darlings.

Act then said to them "Hi you are both lovely."

"Hi Act" the two fairies chorused

Red tip looked at both Susan and Act and said "We have never met people before you look like us only bigger."

"Your clothes are so lovely do you make them yourselves?" Susan asked eagerly

Yellow Tip answered. "Yes we do."

What about your tiny shoes do you make them too?"

Yellow Tip answered crossly. "No don't be silly the Elves make them for us."

Oak-ley interrupted rudely "Why don't you three go to the small clearing just over there," she pointed the way with one of her branches, "I have something very important to talk over with the dragons."

Act told Susan to go ahead Yellow Tip led the way and the three of them walked, skipped and flew to the clearing.

Chapter Thirty-Six

A Plan Emerges.

Once the fairies and Susan were out of earshot Oak-ley couldn't contain herself any longer she bursts out.

"I am sorry about being so abrupt but I have been at my wits end. I have some bad news to tell you." She made them aware of everything she knew and of what she believed was happening, then went on to say. "I have spent most of my time trying to think of ways to contact you. I'm so glad that you are here. The Unicorns are not in any immediate danger but there are lots of animals who are, many have already been killed."

Act said tenderly "Oak-ley there is no need to be sorry I can't imagine how you must have been feeling, not being able to contact the green dragon and with all this on your mind. We are all here now, thank you for sending Susan and the fairies away, they would have been very upset to hear all that terrible news."

Oak-ley replied "Thank you for your consideration.

King turned to Oak-ley and asked "Can you pinpoint the location where the Manhawks are?"

Oak-ley quickly answered "Yes I can, it's on the other side of Pangreat, the rampage is growing daily but it seems to be concentrated, creating a small corridor across the land."

King questioned Oak-ley further. "You told us that you can talk to the animals, can other trees also talk to them?"

Oak-ley said simply "Yes they can."

"The trees in and around the immediate vicinity need to be told to move all the animals away."

"What a good idea I should have thought of that" said Oak-ley feeling more concerned. She closed her eyes whilst she sent her thoughts out to all the trees that needed to know.

King said to both Re-ad and Act "There are a few things on our side, one is the great distance and the other is time, and we have friends who could help us."

Everyone was silent for a short time not knowing what else to say. They hadn't noticed Oak-ley opening her eyes, her deep rich voice broke the silence. "I have given the instructions to evacuate the animals nearest to the Manhawks. I hope that a large enough area along the projected corridor will be void of animals in as quick a time as it takes the slowest to get away."

King remarked confidently "That's good Oak-ley I think that the strategy could prove to be more successful than I first thought."

"Why do you think that?" asked Re-ad.

King looked at Re-ad and then towards Oak-ley and said "Well the fewer animals that are left in the area the less food will be available for the Manhawks to hunt."

Re-ad interrupted "They will get very hungry and eventually get weaker and could starve."

"That's seems a bit extreme!" Oak-ley replied rather shocked.

"I'm sorry Oak-ley I didn't think of that at the time. It's not a nice prospect but it's the only thing I could think of to save the animals. I doubt if any of the Manhawks will starve." He quickly changed the subject and asked her "Has anything like this happened before?"

Oak-ley replied "No nothing on this scale."

Act decided to go and talk to Susan and the fairies, and left the two dragons talking with Oak-ley. Act said "Goodbye" to Oak-ley and walked away.

Oak-ley called out "Goodbye see you in the morning."

Act was glad of the distraction of being in the company of her daughter and the two fairies, she even started to enjoy their company. Susan was so happy she started humming, the fairies joined in, the three sounded so lovely together.

Oak-ley and the two dragons spent a little longer discussing the problem without coming to any decisions King told Oak-ley "We will go back to the farm tomorrow and talk to Grambold I am sure he will be able to tell us something about these Manhawks."

Oak-ley went quiet for a while reflecting about all that had been said and the decisions that were made. Then she said in her usual deep calm voice. "I hope you are right I agree with our intervention, there must be a balance of life and the Manhawks in their pursuit of the Unicorns are upsetting that balance and it's also a worry why they are seeking the Unicorns."

King reassured her, "By the time we return in a few days' time I am sure the news will have improved."

Oak-ley replied "I hope so."

King calmly said "Unfortunately until we know why the Manhawks are after the Unicorns we can do no more about that part."

Sunny and Blue said together, "We should call it a day and get some rest, things always seem better in the morning.

Both dragons turned and started to walk away all wished Oak-ley a "Goodnight."

She replied "I am so relieved that you are here goodnight."

They walked to the clearing in silence but their mood soon changed on seeing the fairies playing with Act and Susan. The fairies joviality and sense of fun raised the dragons spirits, within no time they had joined in the fun and games.

Sunny and Blue thought to one another how guilty they felt about enjoying themselves at such a bad time. Both agreed that it was for Susan's benefit so it was okay. An hour sped by so when Act mentioned. "It's time we called it a day you fairies need to get along to Oak-ley"

Susan just looked at the fairies and said "Thank you for such a lovely time I'll see you in the morning goodnight"

Red Tip and Yellow Tip waved at everyone and flitted back towards Oak-ley.

Act passed the food around, they all ate supper, Susan was chattering happily with her mother. The sun had begun to set and they entered the cave.

The cave was not very big Re-ad went in first and lay out along the back of the cave. Susan and Act took up position in front of her and the green dragon was forced to locate himself with the majority of his body protruding outside the cave. Fortunately it did not rain that night and they all slept very well.

The sun came up and a ray of light shone into the green dragon's eyes and he woke up. He stood up and watched as the sun rose. Susan and Act came and stood by him.

Act remarked. "What a beautiful sight and those sounds coming from the woods are so different from the noises around the farm."

Re-ad came and stood next to them commenting. "Yes it's the morning chorus and lots of animals are joining in too."

They ate breakfast and Act told Susan to go and spend some time with the fairies, she didn't need telling twice Susan skipped all the way. Five sets of eyes watched as she approached.

Oak-ley saw her coming and she called to her. "Good morning Susan did you sleep well?"

Susan answered. "Yes I did thank you how about you?"

Oak-ley could not tell her the truth, it might possibly raise suspicion to what was happening "Not too bad thank you, I know you've come to see the fairies but just like most children they find it hard to get up early in the morning Go inside and try to wake them up. I'm sure they will want to play with you."

Re-ad the green dragon and Act stayed near the cave and discussed some of the problems they may have to face.

King stated "We have to wait and see if the Manhawks get close to the Unicorns before we make any firm decisions, and once we talk to Grambold then we can begin to plan. They stayed around the cave so that Susan could spend more time with the fairies.

Act told them "Susan has had such a lovely time but I think we should be getting back"

The three of them walked slowly towards Oak-ley and chorused together "Good morning."

Sunny and Blue enquired if she'd had a peaceful night.

Oak-ley gave a small yawn. "No not really I kept getting reports from trees relaying the noises being made by the animals as they moved away from the Manhawks. It was a constant, tramping, stomping, slithering and crunching. I am not used to all this activity during the night. It's normally so quiet, eventually I had to shut all the thoughts off to get some sleep."

"You might need to do that every night. Hopefully from today the numbers of killings should reduce." King replied.

She responded enthusiastically "I do hope so."

Act was worried about Susan and the fairies she asked "Can we change the subject. I am concerned in case Susan comes out and hears what we are saying."

King agreed "Yes you are right Act we need to change the subject. He turned to Oak-ley and said. "I don't think you should mention it to the fairies either it may frighten them."

They tried to spend time talking about incidental things, the green dragon was normally never short of words but he found it quite difficult.

Sunny and Blue said awkwardly "Life on the farm has changed so much with the family helping and the size of the community seems to grow daily."

It was proving to be increasingly uncomfortable trying to talk about random things. Sunny and Blue could not continue and impatiently said "Do you think we should get back to the farm?"

Act agreed and shouted for Susan to come and join them.

Red Tip and Yellow Tip both came flying out closely followed by Susan, who said happily.

"Mummy I have had such a lovely time. The only way it could have been any better was if Tame had been here, she would have loved it."

Act looked at Susan and commented. "Your right she would, maybe the next time, we'll see."

"Oh Mummy you always say that" Susan replied

Susan and Act climbed onto the dragons back and started saying their goodbyes to the fairies and Oak-ley.

The two fairies hovered near Oak-ley and waved back. The dragons shouted their "Goodbyes!" as they flew up and away. The wind was at their backs but it still took some four hours before the three peaked mountain loomed into sight.

Chapter Thirty-Seven
A Wonderful Reception

Both dragons landed just outside the barn. Act and Susan climbed down off their backs. Stage, Mark, Tank, Tim and Tame were there to greet them. All the children rushed up to their mother and sister and hugged and kissed them.

Act said jokingly "I need to go away more often this reception is lovely" Stage walked up to Act and put his arms around her in a tender embrace and kissed her. Susan came and snuggled in between them, he kissed Act's ear and whispered. "You're both home safe."

"We were never in any danger and it was good to see Susan having such a wonderful time. You loved it didn't you Susan?"

"Yes and I can't wait till I go again with Tame, Susan answered.

Act pulled away from Stage and said "Now I want to get home to be with my children." She gathered all of them together and walked towards the farmhouse. She turned to Stage and said to him. "Come and see us later when you have had a talk with the two dragons."

Grambold was close by, Sunny and Blue called to him "Will you join us in the barn?"

King turned to Stage and asked him, "Will you come as well?" King didn't wait for an answer he turned to Re-ad and asked her "Do you mind staying out side by the door? we do not want to be disturbed."

Re-ad replied "Okay I can tell anyone who comes to return later."

"Thank you" King said and he walked into the barn followed by Grambold and Stage.

Once they were all inside King looked at Grambold and told him everything that had transpired and what they had done about it. Grambold looked perturbed, he told them everything he knew about the Manhawks. He concluded, "I think the evidence points to a new leader, but I have no idea why he's after the Unicorn Pegasus."

Sunny and Blue outlined the plan that Oak-ley had initiated.

Grambold took a little time to think before he spoke "It could certainly prove to be the right solution. I have often found that some of the best results come from simple plans, but stopping the leader might be the only solution in the end." Grambold pondered a little longer and added "These Manhawks who are looking for the Unicorn will need some kind of leader, high birth Manhawks would not do that, so for the venture to succeed they must have found a solution to the problem."

"So you think their task is possible?" King questioned

Grambold replied "Yes I do it's imperative we keep in contact with Oak-ley. She is the key to this strategy and our early warning once they get close to the Unicorns."

Stage asked "Will we be informing the community?" They agreed not to tell them until it got closer to the time.

Life on the farm continued on very much as before, then a few days later the green dragon took off to see Oak-ley.

Chapter Thirty-Eight
Oak-ley's News

The green dragon landed close to Oak-ley, she was asleep the three heads looked into her face and she woke up. "You landed very quietly I did not hear you coming."

Sunny and Blue said together "What news have you got for us?"

She replied "Thankfully the news is improving there have been fewer animals killed."

"That's really good news" Sunny and Blue said together.

Oak-ley told them, "Some of the Manhawks have been killed, the rest seem to be coming straight towards us which is directly in line to where the Unicorns live. I can predict their route and get most of the animals to move away to the left and the right. The strategy is definitely helping, to reduce the number of deaths. These Manhawks are very resourceful they hunt and forage for anything including creepy crawlies, bugs, fruit, grass and leaves off the trees."

"Well that's bad news if they are heading towards the Unicorns." said Sunny and Blue.

Oak-ley replied "Yes it is and if they keep going in the same direction we will have to do something to keep the Unicorns safe."

King answered "Keeping the Unicorns safe is our top priority."

"Have you got a plan?" Oak-ley asked.

"Grambold has given us lots of information about these Manhawks I think that when it gets closer to the time we need to move the Unicorn Pegasus to a place of safety."

Oak-ley replied "That makes a lot of sense have you somewhere in mind?"

King looked at the other two heads and replied "Yes I thought that Re-ads den would be ideal."

"Have you found a way I can keep in touch with you?" asked Oak-ley

"The only way we can keep in touch is for Re-ad or us to visit you every week to get an update on the Manhawks progress does that sound okay to you?" King asked

Oak-ley sounded more confident "Yes that does seem like a very good plan I am feeling better already." She closed her eyes and nodded off to sleep. The Green dragon walked away as quietly as possible. They shared the food they had brought with them and entered the cave for a nap.

A few hours later they emerged and chatted to Oak-ley for a short time. They waved goodbye and headed back to the farm.

On the return journey they discussed the need to fly faster, and practised different wing shapes and a variety of flapping techniques to increase their speed and were surprised by the results. They were going much faster, so fast the three peaked mountain suddenly appeared below them. The green dragon had to come to an abrupt stop to allow him to glide down and landed just outside the barn.

"Well!" said Sunny and Blue "If and when we need to get to the Manhawks on the other side of Pangreat we'll get there much faster. What we will need, is a map to show us the way Grambold should be able to help with that."

Several children came running up shouting "They are back they are back"

Grambold rushed over to see them and asked excitedly. "Have you good news from Oak-ley?"

King turned to the children and said "Will you let us talk to Grambold? Sorry it's grown up stuff."

The children scurried off and took the others with them who had also come to greet the green dragon. Grambold was then joined by Re-ad Act and Stage. When the children were out of earshot Sunny and Blue answered Grambold's question "Yes! some good news and some bad."

Chapter Thirty-Nine

The Community are Told

King highlighted the news of the emerging plan, and said to Re-ad "I hope you don't mind me suggesting the use of your cave?"

Re-ad agreed "No I don't mind it is the safest place for them."

Nine months passed by and the news from Oak-ley had not changed except that the Manhawks were getting closer to the Unicorns. On Re-ad's last visit Oak-ley estimated that they were two months from the Unicorns location.

Meanwhile back on Millers Farm everyone who was involved discussed the options and the finer details of the plan.

Re-ad had an idea and she put it to King "I think you should take me to meet Grath, Rock, and also the Unicorns so that I'll know how to find them when the time comes.

King agreed, and early next morning as the sun was rising both dragons flew off.

A short time later they arrived at Rock's house, and King introduced them to one another.

Re-ad was some what surprised at his size and his dirty appearance. Sunny and Blue became impatient because it was going to be a busy day, and soon told Rock about the danger the Unicorns were to face in two months' time.

Without any hesitation he said loudly "You can count on me," and with a grimace on his face he thumped his right fist into the palm of his left hand.

The two dragons left Rock and journeyed on, they arrived at Grath's waterfall cave.

Re-ad was impressed with the beauty of the surroundings in particular the thundering waterfall.

Grath was in the pool having a wash, he saw the dragons when they landed but he ignored them for some time busying himself with his bathing.

King called "Grath come out and meet Re-ad."

Grath reluctantly slowly dragged himself out on all fours and joined the dragons.

Introductions were made and King told him about the danger the Unicorns would be facing.

Grath responded in his usual grumpy way and was not very forthcoming and seemed to spend sometime thinking about it.

Re-ad quietly said "Rock the giant has already agreed to come and help"

On hearing this Grath replied "If he's going count me in, one thing how will I get there?"

Re-ad answered "I'll come for you, will you be okay to ride on my back?"

Grath's eyes lit up and excitedly said "I can't wait when will you be coming for me?"

Sunny and Blue replied "In about two months."

On their departure Grath could be seen waving his arms in the air and jumping up and down.

King was pleased and remarked "With those two on board we will not need any other help."

They were headed out to meet the Unicorns. It did not take long before the clearing in the wood came into view, the two of them landed right in the middle of the large grassed circle.

Sunny and Blue called for the Unicorn "Hello will you come out we need to talk to you." The Unicorn walked out of the wood and stopped in front of the green dragon.

King introduced him to Re-ad.

Re-ad was astounded by the magical aura of the Unicorn and in a soft voice said "I am so pleased to meet you." The Unicorn stomped his foot and nodded his head in response.

Sunny and Blue then told the Unicorn why they were visiting him and what they planned to do to help. The Unicorn was grateful but of course he could not relay his feelings to the green dragon so he nodded his head.

King told him "We will see you in about two months and take you both to a safe place will that be okay?"

The Unicorn nodded his head.

"We need to get back to the farm" King concluded.

Both dragons said their farewells and took off and some hours later landed back at Millers Farm.

The following day King decided to inform everyone in the community. Word was put out that a community meeting would be held the next day at midday to coincide with Grambold's lesson.

Everyone turned up and King addressed the crowd "Thank you all for coming this will not take long." He went on to tell them of the danger that the Unicorns were facing and of the final plan they intended to initiate to save them. He finished off by saying "You have nothing to worry about. None of you will be in any danger and you will not be needed to help you will be safe here."

Some of the younger men pushed to the front. A spokes person said bravely "Do you need any fighters we want to help?"

King replied "Thank you brave men for your offer we already have enough old friends to help, besides where we intend to confront the Manhawks is several weeks walk for you. If you really want to help give a hand in the mill and on the farm so we won't have to worry about everything here."

The young men nodded their heads earnestly talking to one another. The spokesperson spoke again. "Most of the people know me I'm Stance we will do as you ask don't worry we will look after everybody when you go."

Sunny and Blue said "That has really put our minds at rest the community will be in good hands thank you." The green dragon started to clap and so did Re-ad followed by the rest of the family. Some of the young men blushed and they all started to filter into the crowd.

King concluded "When It's time for us to go we will let you know. Thank you all for your time and understanding." The crowd dispersed and the family returned to their normal work routine.

Chapter Forty
The Plan is Put into Action

Six weeks later Oak-ley informed Re-ad that the Manhawks were two weeks away from the Unicorns location. Re-ad flew back to the farm in double quick time using the same technique that King had told her about. On landing she told the green dragon the news, then they informed the community.

Both dragons spent a few days stocking up Re-ad's cave with food and water in preparation for the two Unicorns.

On the third day both dragons filled up with oil and gas and fitted the sparklight. Re-ad and the green dragon flew across the sea and landed close to Oak-ley.

King immediately asked her "Are the Manhawks still heading towards the Unicorns?"

Oak-ley replied "Yes they are. I think they are less than a week away from the Unicorns location, you need to get them out as quickly as you can."

King answered "We will, I've been thinking that the fairies would all be safer here with you what do you think?"

Oak-ley simply said "Yes you are right I had thought about it and I am sure if you ask them they will come with you."

The green dragon took the lead and landed where the fairies lived. Sunny and Blue called out "Red Tip, Yellow Tip, Blue Tip where are you?" Within a few moments they were flitting around the three heads eager to play.

Sunny and Blue introduced them to Re-ad "Hi" she said gently "It's lovely to meet you."

The three fairies were shy and looked furtively at Re-ad with out saying a word.

King spoke softly "Come on you three say hello, she is our friend"

They all called out in their sweet voices "Hello Re-ad"

Re-ad acknowledged them with a nod of her head saying "Now I understand why Susan loves you, you're so very beautiful"

King spoke urgently. "The Unicorns are in danger, we have to take them to a place of safety and need you three to come along. You can show us the quickest way!"

Sunny then added "When we come back here all the fairies can join us and we'll take you to stay with Oak-ley. Think of it as one big adventure."

Red Tip hovered near King and called "Okay follow us"

The green dragon and Re-ad tried to follow them, but the fairies flew really low dodging in and out of tree branches.

King called them "Hi little ones we are finding it hard to keep up with you. Will you sit on our heads and direct us?" Red Tip sat on Kings head, Blue Tip sat on Blue and Yellow Tip fluttered over to Sunny.

The green dragon was followed by Re-ad who flew up over the tree tops as the fairies called out the directions. Within a short while they were gliding down to land in the clearing.

King asked Red Tip to call for the Unicorns which she did and within a few minutes both the Unicorns appeared walking towards them.

Red Tip flew over to the male Unicorn, listened to his thoughts and told King they were both ready to leave.

King spoke to the Unicorn. "We will guide you both to a place of safety. We will also take the fairies to stay with Oak-ley they will be safe with her."

Yellow Tip listened to the male Unicorn's thoughts and she repeated them "He thanks you for your help."

Sunny and Blue were anxious to get going and beckoned the Unicorns to follow them.

The fairies sat back onto the dragon heads as he flew up. They all soon landed where the fairies lived.

Red Tip, Yellow Tip and Blue Tip called and all the fairies came out. Some climbed onto the green dragon some onto Re-ad and some onto the two Unicorn's backs.

They all took off and after travelling some distance needed to stop to give the Unicorns a rest. They started on the next leg of the journey and eventually arrived near Oak-ley. All the fairies flew into her canopy.

Oak-ley was so happy to see the Unicorns and exclaimed, "You are in good hands the dragons will do everything in their power to keep you safe."

King then told the Unicorns "Rest for as long as you need, nod and stamp your leg when you are ready to fly and nay when you need to land."

Both Unicorns nodded their heads and stomped their front legs. They all took off and waved goodbye to Oak-ley who in turn shouted "Good luck."

They stopped several times along the way and had to rest over night. The following day they came down to land just outside Re-ad's cave.

Re-ad led them inside and showed them around "Make yourselves at home there is food and water here for you. What we have to do should not take long but you might have to stay here several weeks until we come for you are you happy with that?" The male Unicorn stomped his leg and nodded his head. Re-ad then said "It's imperative we leave now so goodbye."

The green dragon was waiting for her out side and said "Come on we need to get going." They both took off flew across the sea and eventually went in different directions putting the next stage of the plan into action.

Chapter Forty-One

Fight With the Manhawks

Re-ad located Grath, who was really excited and couldn't wait to climb onto Re-ad's back.

"Hold on tight" Re-ad shouted. Grath was exhilarated by the speed and called out in high pitched sounds.

Re-ad called to him "Calm down your making a terrible noise it's hurting my ears" He stopped but couldn't sit still for more than a minute.

Meanwhile the green dragon arrived near Rock's house. Sunny and Blue shouted "Rock!" as they were about to land.

Rock came running out calling "Don't bother landing I'm ready. I'll follow you."

Rock ran very fast behind the green dragon taking massive strides and great leaps. He called out "Hi can't you go any faster?" They increased their speed and were surprised to see Rock keeping up with them.

By night fall the four were standing in the middle of the large circle discussing how they would tackle the Manhawks. Their position gave them an all round clear view. Re-ad and the green dragon took up positions facing the general direction where the Manhawks were expected to come from. Grath and Rock stood either side of the dragons in case the Manhawks approached from the sides.

Sunny and Blue said "We need to capture the leader, he'll be the one in front of the group and giving the orders."

Re-ad calmly said "Leave him to me I know exactly how to deal with him."

King said "Remember it is not our intention to kill any of them so please bear this in mind when the fighting begins."

Just in case the Manhawks changed their strategy it was decided that they should keep watch through the night, each took it in turns. The green dragon was awake as the sun came up because it was his watch, the other three were woken by the sun shining on their faces. There was a stillness in the air It was eerie and quiet, there were no birds singing or even crickets chirping. Everyone looked around nobody said a word.

The silence was broken by a cry that was made by one of the Manhawks as he ran out of the wood. He came across the open grassed space and advanced towards the two dragons. He stopped in his tracks as both stood up and loomed over him. A line of Manhawks started to emerge from the wood behind him.

Re-ad reacted very quickly. She knocked the leader of the group to the ground, grasped him in her rear claws and flew straight up into the sky. She called to him "Are you the leader?"

Simultaneously the green dragon had moved quickly forward so allowing Sunny and Blue to breathe a flaming barrier across the Manhawk's path. One of the Manhawks was set alight and thrashed about wildly, most of the Manhawks were forced to stop in front of the flames. They started to shoot arrows at the green dragon but they just bounced off. Some arrows were aimed at Rock but to him they were so small he didn't even notice.

Two of the Manhawks who were trapped on the wrong side of the flames were stamped on by Rock and unfortunately were killed. He also gripped several in his large hands.

One is attacked by Grath who kept him pinned down.

Meanwhile the Manhawk trapped in Re-ad's claws replied in a frightened voice "Yes I am Featherhawk the leader."

Re-ad warned him "If you do not do as I say I will pluck your wings out and drop you to your death, do you understand?"

Featherhawk replied now even more frightened, "Yes I understand what do you want me to do?"

Re-ad ordered him "Tell all the Manhawks to put down their weapons and stop fighting we do not want to kill any of you. Do it now!"

Featherhawk screamed as loudly as he could "Manhawks stop! Manhawks put your weapons down."

King shouted even louder "Manhawks stop fighting put your weapons down."

Slowly the Manhawks stopped fighting their weapons were dropped to the ground. Sunny and Blue ceased breathing fire.

Re-ad placed Featherhawk down and landed next to him. The remainder of the Manhawks were ushered together and commanded to stand by Featherhawk.

Grath started to collect all the weapons and stacked them in a pile out of the way.

King looked at Featherhawk and asked him. "Why are you after the Unicorn?"

"We are to take back the magical horn to our leader because he said its powers will make us fly" Featherhawk replied.

Sunny and Blue stated abruptly "That is not the power of the horn your leader is misinformed we know that it's got the power to heal, not to help anyone fly. You need to go back and tell your leader this information."

King asked "What is your leaders name?"

Featherhawk answered "Bravehawk is his name and he will not believe me when I tell him what you say"

King responded "Then we will have to go and talk to him in person perhaps he will believe us."

Re-ad asked thoughtfully "What will we do with these Manhawks?" Standing with Featherhawk are only seven others.

King told them "You will never find the Unicorn in his new hiding place. If we let you go will you promise to return home?"

The eight survivors talked amongst themselves and Featherhawk replied "We have no other choice so we will do as you say."

King looked at Rock and asked him. "Will you accompany them to make sure they start back? Re-ad can then take Grath home, I need to talk to Oak-ley."

Rock nodded his head and said "I'll go with them until midday I want to get home before it gets too dark."

King replied "Thank you for all your help" and then warned the Manhawks "Remember this. We were waiting for you because we knew exactly where to find you. We will also know if you try to come back or deviate from your way home."

Rock added loudly "Come on let's get you on your way." The eight Manhawks moved out going back the way they came. Rock walked along behind them.

Blue and Sunny turned to Grath and said "Thank you for your help we made a great team."

Re-ad called Grath over to her and he eagerly climbed onto her back and she flew off and shouted to the green dragon "See you back at the farm."

Chapter Forty-Two

Home For a Short Rest

The green dragon also took off and headed back to see Oak-ley. He told her what had happened and why the Manhawks were after the Unicorn. He informed Oak-ley "Re-ad and I will have to go and visit Bravehawk we can not have a repeat of this again. The strange thing is the Unicorn unknowingly was the cause of the trouble but ultimately could end up being a solution to the problem."

Oak-ley replied "That sounds rather complicated."

King said jokingly "Do not worry Oak-ley I intend to use a bit of trickery. Keep the fairies with you until next week and we'll come and see you then to make sure the Manhawks are still heading home."

She was so relieved and said "Thank goodness you were able to help. Get on home to your family see you next week."

King replied "We could not have done it with out the help of Re-ad, Grath and Rock"

The green dragon said their goodbyes and flew up and headed for home. On the way they discussed the new plan, a few things needed to be ironed out with Grambold's help.

All the community had gathered around as the green dragon landed.

King informed them that the plan worked well "Re-ad will be here soon. We'll then have a good rest and spend some time with our family."

Together the whole family surrounded the dragon and ushered him into the barn. The people outside reluctantly dispersed.

Re-ad landed only a few minutes later, the barn door opened. Susan ran out and beckoned Re-ad inside.

The two dragons were made to sit together as food and tankards of beer were brought for them. Everyone was so happy that they were home safely. The family sang together the atmosphere was very jovial.

King sipped his beer and commented. "What a welcome party this is so thoughtful of you all."

Sunny and Blue said "We will not tell you the whole grisly story." Between them they related a rough outline of the events. Re-ad had her input at the appropriate time they were all in awe of their exploits.

Act had been studying the two dragons for a short while. She suddenly announced "Okay everyone these tired dragons need a good night's sleep let's get out of here so they can get some well earned rest."

The dragons sleepily in turn replied "Goodnight"

Stage closed the barn door behind him and the two dragons fell asleep where they lay.

The following day the green dragon took Grambold to one side King asked him "Can you produce a map showing the way to the Manhawks flock?"

Grambold answered "Yes I can it will take a few days. Have you got a plan?"

King had a rough plan in his mind and put it to them. "We need to fly out and see Bravehawk that's for sure. My idea is to ask the Unicorn if we can use a small piece of his horn to turn Bravehawk from bad to good, and then to trick him into taking it in the hope that it will make him fly, what do you think?"

Grambold responded "Brilliant simply brilliant you are only giving him what he wants, you might have to tell a few small lies but it should work."

When do you intend to start the trip Sunny and Blue asked.

King replied "Once the Unicorns are safely home."

Over the next few days both dragons related the events of the fight with the Manhawks to most of the community. They all listened intently and had great admiration for the brave few who took part.

Grambold had completed the map and handed it over to the green dragon, informing him that he had recorded the past events in his book.

King thanked him and asked "Have you anything else to add to my plan?"

When you arrive outside their caves you need to shock Bravehawk. Perhaps a flame demonstration would do the trick."

Before the week was out Re-ad flew out to see Oak-ley. She came back the same day with good news that the Manhawks were still heading home.

At the end of the week the green dragon flew to see the Unicorns and asked "Can I have a scraping off your horn I want it for the leader of the Manhawks I am hoping it will make him good. Can it do that?"

The Unicorn stomped and nodded his head.

Sunny and Blue asked "Will it hurt"

The Unicorn shook its head.

King was still as gentle as he could be, he used a sharp talon and took a very thin short piece and placed it into a small pouch that he tied around his neck.

Another week later the green dragon and Re-ad topped up with oil, gas and fitted the sparklight. They then visited Oak-ley the news was even better.

Oak-ley told them "I sent the fairies home yesterday the Manhawks are well on their way home. I think it would be safe for the Unicorns to go home too. I'm intrigued about your trickery can you tell me what you intend to do?"

King explained "I have got some scrapings off the Unicorn's magical horn. The trick is to make him eat the scraping."

Oak-lay was astonished by the plan and asked "I assume you'll only take enough for one dose? and your relying on his vanity and greed to take it himself, it's very clever."

Blue and Sunny answered "By the time the potion works on him he will not be aware that he has been tricked. We have decided to go and take the Unicorns back home."

Both dragons stayed the night in the cave then flew to Re-ads cave the following day.

The Unicorns seemed to be happy with the outcome of the Manhawks and were keen to return home.

Sunny and Blue asked the Unicorns "Shall we fly home with you?"

They shook their heads indicating no. The green dragon and Re-ad said "Goodbye" and the two Unicorns ran along and took off.

Chapter Forty-Three
Arriving at the Manhawks Mountain

Once the Unicorns were out of sight both dragons flew up together. They flew higher than they had ever flown before and seemed to catch a very strong fast wind which was blowing in the general direction they wanted to go. They obtained super speeds and used the wind to glide whilst taking rests.

At the end of the first day they had travelled a huge distance they landed and ate some of the food they had brought with them. As dawn broke the next day they picked up the strong tail wind. They didn't need to refer to Grambold's map they could remember every detail.

After flying for three more days Sunny and Blue remarked to Re-ad "This is the longest that we have had gas and oil in our tummy and for some reason we do not seem to be getting hungry. Do you feel the same?"

Re-ad replied "Yes I do but I never did eat much before we met. I only started to eat more after I discarded the oil and gas I never gave it any thought."

King thoughtfully replied "The oil and gas must be feeding us and giving us energy."

Seven days later they could see in the distance the mountain where the Manhawks lived.

King commented "It's just as Grambold described it."

On the far side of the old volcano they saw the caves where the Manhawks lived so they landed on open ground just in front of them. Manhawks appeared out of the caves and advanced slowly towards them not knowing what to do.

King called out in his loudest voice "Bravehawk Bravehawk we come in peace and have something very special for you."

The Manhawks moved aside leaving a path to enable Bravehawk to walk towards the dragons. He stopped some way back from them and called out. "I am Bravehawk what have you got for me?"

King answered "Before I tell you that, are your flock about to attack us?"

The flock seemed to be closing in on them.

Bravehawk had been aware of what was happening and he held his hands up in the air and shouted "Stop!" All the Manhawks stopped instantly and Bravehawk in a firm voice said. "My Manhawks follow my orders they will not attack unless I order them to."

Re-ad called out "You need to think twice before you make such an order we are more than capable of looking after ourselves may I demonstrate?" She didn't wait for an answer. A flame of fire shot out of her mouth. All the Manhawks cowered and started to shrink away.

"Stand your ground Manhawks" Bravehawk shouted "That's very impressive" he admitted.

Sunny and Blue looked around checking on the Manhawks. Re-ad was also being very vigilant.

King lowered his head down towards Bravehawk and started to talk in a low voice. "Will you come a little closer? what I have to say are for your ears only."

Bravehawk almost stumbled as he took a hurried step back.

King continued "If I was going to kill you, you'd be dead by now, don't you think?"

Bravehawk regained his composure and walked closer to King so that he could hear Kings' hushed tones.

King in a quiet voice said "I have some scrapings for you that I took from the magical horn of a Unicorn that I believe you are after."

Bravehawk looked directly into King's eyes and said "How did you know that I wanted it?"

King simply looked from side to side as if making sure no one else was listening, "It's a long story, the details of which you do not need to know, other than we met Featherhawk. He told us that you wanted the Unicorn's horn. He could not find it and is now on his way back to you."

"You lie! How do I know that you did not take it from him?" Bravehawk demanded.

King replied calmly "That's a good question but my answer is simple. If you are happy to wait some nine months to find out the truth then fine, we will be on our way."

King pulled away and shouted loudly "Our business is finished here we need to get back home"

The green dragon started to walk away.

Bravehawk panicked and shouted abruptly "No wait! come back let's talk a little more."

The green dragon returned, King lowered his head to Bravehawk and said "Tell your flock to put down their weapons we do not want to start a war do we?"

Bravehawk responded instantly and called out "Put your weapons on the ground and move away from them." The flock did as they were ordered.

"Have you brought much horn with you?" Bravehawk asked King.

King was ready with a small lie that was part of the trickery "No sorry we didn't think to bring any more, Featherhawk thought it was just for you."

Bravehawk stretched out his arm and opened his hand saying sternly "Give it to me I'll take it now."

King replied "As you wish but you'll need some water to wash it down I'll reduce it to dust for you." King took the small pouch from the string hanging around his neck and emptied the small piece into the palm of his clawed hand and crushed it.

Bravehawk watched intently at the action of the clawed hands crushing its contents "Bring me some water." he ordered.

Shreakhawk ran off and came back with a cup of water. "What are you doing?" she asked.

"It's the mystical horn of the Unicorn, go back where you came from" he ordered her abruptly.

The green dragon trickled the dust into Bravehawk's cupped hand, who carefully placed it into his mouth and gulped the water. A few seconds later and it was all gone. Nothing happened for a while then Bravehawk fell onto his knees.

The Manhawks started to rush forward to pick up their weapons.

King shouted out "Manhawks stop! Bravehawk is alright"

Bravehawk stood up and looked around wondering what had happened. He ran off a little way flapping his wings. "What am I doing? why am I trying to fly?" he said surprised at himself. Then he commanded "Our guests must be hungry get some food and drink for them come we will sit together and talk about your journey."

Cordial chatter took place and Bravehawk asked the dragons to spend the night with them.

Sunny and Blue graciously accepted. Later that day Shreakhawk managed to get the green dragon alone and asked "What have you done to Bravehawk? he is so considerate even, dare I say it, kind."

"We just gave him what he has always wanted, some Unicorn magic, would you prefer the old Bravehawk back?" Sunny and Blue answered sheepishly

Shreakhawk hurriedly replied "No no the flock will now prosper and grow under our leadership thank you."

In the morning during breakfast King asked Bravehawk "Can I offer you a small piece of advice? for the well being of your flock."

Bravehawk nodded his head and said "I will take any advice you give me very seriously, what is it?"

"Keep your flock together" King stated."

Bravehawk replied "That is good advice."

After breakfast the two dragons topped up with oil and flew off waving goodbye. The journey back took longer because they had to fly below the strong wind current that previously helped them.

Thirteen days later they glided down and landed just beside Oak-ley. She was glad to see them and so pleased that it all went to plan.

She informed them "The small group of Manhawks are well on their way home. The animals are returning to their homes."

They stayed over night said goodbye to Oak-ley and were glad to be heading back to the farm.

The welcome home was warm and friendly the family were the first to greet them. People rushed to the farm to see them and the two dragons decided to tell the story there and then.

The community spent days discussing the adventure. Grambold entered it into his book.

Life on the farm and within the community soon settled back to the normal routine.

Chapter Forty-Four
Visit to the Volcano

Six weeks later Blue and Sunny mentioned to Re-ad "We were hoping to go and visit the Unicorns and as you told us the volcano was not too far away from where they live, we hoped you would show us the way."

Re-ad was not too happy but said "Okay I'll show you where the volcano is, when do you want to go?"

King answered "Let's go today."

Re-ad took the lead and after several hours of very fast flying Re-ad brought them down some distance from the volcano.

Sunny and Blue said to Re-ad "Stay here we'll come back when we've had a look around."

Re-ad called after them "Please be careful."

The green dragon took off and flew up over the lip of the volcano and was surprised to see how big it was inside.

King was intrigued by the scorched landscape he exclaimed excitedly "It looks as if several dragons have been breathing fire everywhere it must have been extremely hot in there."

The inside of the crater was so big he was able to glide effortlessly around the whole perimeter. The three heads seemed to be drawn into the crater and slowly glided further down into the massive cavernous bowl shaped interior.

Without any warning there was an explosion, followed instantly by a large plume of smoke and expanding gases that shot out from its centre core.

The green dragon instinctively responded by flapping its wings as fast as possible trying to gain height and turned away from the expanding smoke and gasses.

Another even louder bang shot out flames, bits of molten lava and chunks of rock. The once very large space inside the crater was suddenly reduced in size due to the amount of swirling smoke and steam.

Blue and Sunny cooperated together and positioned their heads and necks to protect King from the flying debris.

Re-ad reacted when she heard the first explosion, she flew up as fast as she could until she heard the second bang and decided to fly even higher and further away from the volcano. When she was out of danger she stopped and turned around hovering. She looked down at the explosion and the damage it had caused. Rocks and pieces of molten lava were tossed out of the volcano like toys.

Molten lava started to flow down the far side of the volcano.

Re-ad didn't want to think about what could have happened to the green dragon. Then she glimpsed a faint outline appearing out of the smoke.

She rushed down and called out "Thank goodness, you are okay."

Kings voice could hardly be heard above the sounds of the roaring volcano "We must land something is wrong with Sunny and Blue."

Re-ad shouted with a fearful response "No! No! we must get further away." She could see that the green dragon was having problems flying and positioned herself underneath him and took as much of his weight as she could.

King called out "Re-ad I must land move away I'll glide down."

Re-ad reluctantly pulled away. Going down faster than normal he crashed into the ground landing rather badly. The wings were left out tattered and torn with gaping holes in them.

Re-ad landed and stood beside King. He said in a very quiet voice "Something is very wrong with Sunny and Blue can you see how they are?"

Re-ad was shocked to see that both necks were covered in bloody wounds. Sunny and Blue had shards of rock embedded in their heads. She feared the worst tears ran down her face.

King whispered to her as she came closer to him. "I am feeling weaker" his eyes closed and he slipped into unconsciousness.

Re-ad screamed "No No!" and shot off into the sky as fast as she could. She knew what to do and within minutes she landed where the Unicorns lived and pleaded with them, "Please the green dragon needs your help" The male Unicorn nodded his head and ran taking off. Re-ad joined him and led the way.

She landed near the green dragon afraid to look at him.

The Unicorn landed and came to an abrupt stop just beside the green dragon He lowered his head and tapped each head in turn with his magical horn, sparks flickered and a bright light came from each of their heads. The light travelled down each neck and along the body into the wings. It continued to travel throughout the dragons body and when it reached the tip of his tail the light went out.

King Blue and Sunny then opened their eyes. All the wounds had been healed and the tattered wings were whole again. The shards of rock miraculously fell out of their heads.

Re-ad said "Take it easy the Unicorn has healed your injuries."

King looked at the Unicorn and said clearly "Thank you so much you saved our lives."

Sunny and Blue also said "Thank you we are so grateful for what you have done."

At that moment the Unicorn was thinking "I am only paying back what you did for me"

The green dragon got up and stroked the Unicorn who then nodded his head.

Re-ad said "We should accompany the Unicorn home." But the Unicorn shook his head indicating no, he ran and took off. Both dragons waved and called out. "Goodbye."

Chapter Forty-Five
Games in the Snow

Both dragons flew off to Re-ad's cave for a few days to rest up. The following day the green dragon and Re-ad were out side the cave admiring the snow covered peak when Sunny and Blue said eagerly "We were wondering if it would be a good time to fly up and see the snow it looks so beautiful."

Re-ad looked up towards the mountain and answered "Yes it does but, it can change very quickly" she scanned the sky for a while and eventually nodded her head, "It looks clear everywhere we can go now."

King called out excitedly "That's great we'll follow you Re-ad."

After circling and climbing slowly somewhat like eagles using the hot rising thermals, Re-ad eventually brought them in to land on a large flat outcrop, that was located a short distance below the summit.

Re-ad said "This is the best location up here, there is plenty of room to walk around and experience the snow."

The green dragon began to toss claws full of snow in the air and without any warning large chunks of virgin snow were thrown at

Re-ad.

She didn't react immediately but as he persisted with the childlike game she decided to retaliate and gathered a load of snow and aimed it at the three heads. All three heads managed to dodge it and in their excitement dived and slithered along the snow resembling a penguin as he slid along on his tummy.

When he came to a stop Re-ad who had made some compressed snowballs in her claws, tossed one and hit King on the nose.

On seeing this Sunny and Blue burst out with laughter.

Then Re-ad using both hands threw snow balls at both of them and they landed right on target hitting Blue and Sunny at the same time.

King laughed even louder and shouted to Re-ad "Hey that's quite some feat how many hands have you got?"

"Come on lets get her" Sunny and Blue called out playfully. The green dragon took hold of Re-ad and swung her around and then released her.

She slid along the snow packed surface and ended up buried head first into a large snow drift, only her tail remained visible.

King panicked and called out in concern "Re-ad! Re-ad! are you alright?"

He rushed over and gently took hold of her

tail and started to pull her slowly out of the snow.

Unknown to them Re-ad was unhurt. She used the time under the snow to make three big snowballs. Just as she was freed from the snow she spun around quickly and plopped a snow ball directly onto each of the three heads. "That suites you really well" she shouted laughing at the same time.

Sunny, Blue and King looked at each other and the three of them laughed at what they saw.

King uttered "You had us all worried you trickster"

Just then snow flakes started to drift down. The green dragon stood in awe and held out both arms. Three necks stretched up their heads tilted back, causing the snowballs to drop off their heads. They opened their mouths and stuck out their tongues to catch the snow flakes.

King glanced down to Re-ad and said excitedly "This is something really special."

She looked at him and realised that they had made it special just by being there with her.

Something caught her eye. She looked up and saw the wind whipping the snow off the sides and the topmost peak of the mountain. The snow around them was falling much faster now and denser, the wind drove it sideways.

She was worried and called out "We need to get down from here there is a storm on the way."

King looked at her "Storm! isn't he friendly?"

She pointed to the ridge above them that was now lost in a snow blizzard "No it's not"

The blizzard was now blowing against them making moving difficult. King shouted to Re-ad "Get down onto your tummy and use your rear legs to push you along follow us, we'll peel off to the right you go left."

Re-ad did as she was told. They moved off slowly at first heading towards the edge of the outcrop. Both dragons picked up speed and were soon skiing on their tummies as fast as they could.

The green dragon shot off the ledge closely followed by Re-ad who very quickly deployed her wings and started to glide down to the left.

King, Sunny and Blue kept their wings in even though the storm was left well behind them. The three of them were excited and thrilled and became hooked on the adrenalin that the free fall was generating through their veins.

Re-ad looked down to see the green dragon shooting down as if in a death fall.

She tried to catch them up and called out in

panic "Are you okay? please deploy your wings. Are you alright?"

King heard the fear in her voice and realised how worried she must have been. He called to Sunny and Blue "Okay that's enough." The wings came out and they drifted and glided the rest of the way down and landed just outside Re-ad's cave.

When Re-ad joined them King was the first to apologise "Sorry Re-ad we did not mean to scare you but the feeling we had as we fell was so exhilarating the sense of freedom and the speed was wonderful.

Re-ad looked at them crossly "You enjoyed that! that! free falling?"

Sunny and Blue blushed "Sorry Re-ad but yes we did the free falling was so exciting. You must try it next time."

Re-ad didn't know what to say so she just turned around and stomped off and disappeared into her cave.

That night in the cave the three heads talked to Re-ad. She could not stay mad at them for long, as they chattered excitedly of the wonderful time they had spent together playing in the snow.

On the third day King remarked "Come on it's time to get back to the farm."

Ten months have passed and eventually the small group of Manhawks returned home they were given a heroes welcome. The flock would grow and prosper under Bravehawk and Shreakhawks wise rule.

The years go by and the community continued to grow steadily, not just with settlers arriving but, with babies being born. More houses were built and the barn was extended to accommodate the growing dragons. Both have grown to twice the size they used to be. Neither of them can fit in the mill so the work is carried out by Stage. Tank helps and so does Tame who loves working with the grain helping to turn it into flour.

Trampo and Whitestar had five fouls, four of them look like Whitestar and the other one resembled Trampo.

Forward thirty years and life on the farm is very much as it's always been, except for the green dragon and Re-ad who spend a lot of time together. Their size makes it difficult to move safely around people so they tend to live in Re-ad's cave and enjoy being in her lovely quiet valley.

The five children have grown up into well adjusted adults and have families of their own. Either the green dragon or Re-ad take members of the family to visit Myrtle who offers them trips to the bottom of the sea.

Groups of younger children visit and play with the fairies and often stop off to see

Oak-ley. The Unicorn Pegasus are only visited twice a year they like to keep to themselves so their wishes are respected.

Grambold invented the pigeon post and communication is kept with smaller communities who live by the sea and others in far off places. He unfortunately passed away in his sleep at the ripe old age of four hundred and sixty years.

Susan took up his role as teacher and continued to write stories and any facts that she heard about were recorded into Grambold's old book, she soon had to start a new one.

Grambold's vision and legacy goes on and helps the community to prosper. Knowledge is passed on via the written word. Communication helps people of the old world in a specific way and the world seems to be a smaller place because of it.

During those thirty years there has been peace and harmony throughout the community. Grath eventually found a mate and had two young Tuskuns. Rock came and visited Millers Farm to barter with the traders.

Oak-ley keeps reporting that the world is in a good even balance. All is well in the old world.

The End

Acknowledgements

Firstly I have to make a special mention and big thank you to Luke my ten year old grandson, who after I told him a made up story about a three headed dragon said "You should write a book about him granddad".

He was my inspiration and sounding board as the characters developed and the chapters grew in number.

Secondly I thank Sarah a part time cartoonist illustrator who, came to my rescue quite late into the project, she gave life to many of the characters.

Thirdly I must thank Carol my wife for all the proof reading and grammar changes she made. Without all her help and support the book would never have been completed to such a good standard.

Finally I must thank Debbie Williams (no relation) my Australian editor, for her professionalism and understanding, she shaped the content and structure of the manuscript.

Lightning Source UK Ltd.
Milton Keynes UK
UKHW01f0349170518
322674UK00001BA/37/P

9 781787 197046